"I broke

His dad pushed h.... .... last it
tipped over. "What the hell are you talking about,
Cooper?"

"I broke off the engagement. Right before you
called me."

"My God! You and your brother are going to ruin
this family. How could you be so stupid?"

"It didn't have anything to do with the family,
Dad."

"You don't think 'Cheating Senator's Brother
Breaks Heart of Grieving Fiancée' is going to be
a story that gets picked up? Or did you forget
somehow that your wedding is the kick-off event
for the tenth anniversary of the Wish Foundation,
a group that grants goddamn wishes to people
who are dying? How is the governor supposed to
appoint you if you're no better than your brother?"

"Maybe it's a good thing," Cooper said. "I won't be
distracted by Jorie and the wedding. Total focus
for the new job."

He looked to his cousin for support, but Theo
only said, "There's no way, Coop. You're going to
get crucified."

"Get Jorie back," his dad said flatly.

So. It was already starting. The switch from a
private, ordinary life to a life that was a career.
And Jorie had gone from ex-fiancée to business
asset in the span of one afternoon.

Dear Reader,

When I first started writing romance, I thought all of my books would have to end with a wedding. As I learned more about this genre, I realized I was wrong about that. (And many other things!) Romances aren't about marriage, they're about commitment and true love. For some of the fictional couples in my books, a wedding is the right happily ever after, but for some, their commitment to each other may take a different form, at least at the point where the book ends.

This book starts with an engagement, but I wasn't sure how it would end until the last minutes of revision on the last draft before I handed it in. I think life works that way sometimes—it's hard to find the right path, especially when the stakes are high and hearts are involved. I hope you'll have a good time reading along with Jorie and Cooper as they work out their story.

Extras, including behind-the-scenes facts, deleted scenes and information about my other books are on my website at www.ellenhartman.com. Look for other Harlequin Superromance authors and readers on our Facebook page at: www.facebook.com/HarlequinSuperromance. I'd love to hear from you! Send email to ellen@ellenhartman.com.

Ellen Hartman

Married by June
Ellen Hartman

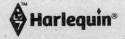

TORONTO NEW YORK LONDON
AMSTERDAM PARIS SYDNEY HAMBURG
STOCKHOLM ATHENS TOKYO MILAN MADRID
PRAGUE WARSAW BUDAPEST AUCKLAND

Recycling programs
for this product may
not exist in your area.

ISBN-13: 978-0-373-71711-8

MARRIED BY JUNE

www.Harlequin.com

Printed in U.S.A.

ABOUT THE AUTHOR

Ellen graduated from Carnegie Mellon with a degree in creative writing and then spent the next fifteen years writing technical documentation. Eventually, she worked up the courage to try fiction and has been enjoying her new career as a romance author.

Currently, Ellen lives in a college town in New York with her husband and sons.

Books by Ellen Hartman

HARLEQUIN SUPERROMANCE
1427—WANTED MAN
1491—HIS SECRET PAST
1563—THE BOYFRIEND'S BACK
1603—PLAN B: BOYFRIEND
1665—CALLING THE SHOTS

I would like to thank my cousin, Mary Beth, who generously provided me with background information I used to imagine Jorie's apartment.

I'd also like to thank my cousin, Carla, who replayed her wedding cake tasting for me so I'd get the details for that scene right.

My critique partners, Christianne, Diana, Leslie, Lisa and Mary, are a source of patient support for me on every book.

Diana gave me key insights on this one— thanks for everything!

PROLOGUE

"MY MOM LOOKED A little better tonight, didn't she?" Jorie asked.

It was a clear night but the D.C. streets were practically empty. Cooper had suggested that he walk her home after their hospital visit, and Jorie was glad he was with her. Her mom was dying. Probably before the year was over, although her doctor had hopes that his latest treatment cocktail would buy a few extra months. It was almost impossible to accept that her mom would soon be gone.

Cooper and his family had met her mom, Chelsea, only a few months ago, but they'd taken her into their hearts. For the first time, Jorie was sharing her mom with other people who loved Chelsea. It felt like a luxury.

Cooper took her hand.

"She got some news today that perked her up," he said.

"What news? Why didn't she tell me?"

"She wanted it to be a surprise."

The spotlights on the front of the Capitol building

glinted in his brown eyes, making them sparkle as he looked down at her. Suddenly he swung in front of her and dropped to one knee. "Jorie, will you marry me?"

"What? No!" she said. The guard halfway up the steps straightened. He held his gun casually in front of his chest, but the Capitol was no place for messing around. "You've got to be—"

"The Wish Team granted your mom's wish," Cooper said, never looking away from her.

"What wish?" Jorie could feel her world starting to spin.

"She wants to give you a princess wedding. The one she's always dreamed of. The Wish Team is picking up the tab—"

"Wait— My wedding? To whom?"

He stood up. She'd hurt him. Well, obviously. She was acting as if he was the last man she'd ever consider marrying when he'd been the one keeping her afloat these past few months. "Oh, God, Coop. I'm sorry. I'm just—this is all…"

Suddenly he took her by the waist and swung her up onto the third step. The stairs made her slightly taller than him, but the difference in perspective didn't do much to calm her. She put her hands on his shoulders to steady herself.

"Jorie, she made this wish for us. I know it sounds

nuts, but as soon as she told me, I knew she was right—the idea is inspired. Marry me."

She couldn't think with him looking up at her, proposing to her. How many times had her mom described this scene to her when she was a little girl? *Someday, Jorie, your prince will ask you to marry him.* Cooper was sweet and smart and funny and gorgeous—everything she'd ever wanted in a guy. She thought she loved him, why wouldn't she love him? But—

"We met six months ago, Cooper," she said, trying to remind herself why she had to say no. "You can't let my mom's schemes get in the way of your good sense. She's obsessed with romance— with weddings—and always has been."

The guard had moved down a few steps, his stance alert. Cooper noticed him for the first time and waved one hand. "I'm proposing!"

"Good luck to you," the guard called back, but he now stood close enough to hear what they said. Cooper put his arm around her shoulders and escorted her across the sidewalk, out of view. He stopped under a streetlight and reached into the breast pocket of his suit. She expected him to come out with a ring box, and when he didn't, she wasn't sure if she should be relieved or disappointed. He handed her a packet of papers.

"Okay, yes. I want to make your mom happy. If

we get married now, she can be there to see it. But I wouldn't be asking you if it wasn't right. I knew you'd say we haven't been together long enough, but if we wait…your mom…"

He couldn't finish, and she realized she wasn't the only one who loved her mom. "I wrote this for you," he said.

She took the little booklet and saw that he'd drawn a picture on the cover. The people in the picture were quick sketches in the spidery black ink she recognized from his fountain pen. The man was about twice as tall as the woman, who had a binder under one arm and a slice of cake in her other hand. She and Cooper, no doubt. He'd drawn a heart around the couple and underneath had written, "To be continued…"

She turned the page and started reading.

It was a fairy tale—the worst kind of romantic nonsense.

Her hands shook as she read each page.

He'd imagined their relationship, the way it would have been if her mom weren't sick. If they waited to get to know each other better, to cross all their bridges and find all their necessary compromises. He was a speechwriter and knew how to pull his reader in with the perfect phrase.

On August 24, I invite you over for dinner. You thought it would be takeout because you've never forgiven me for the frozen pizza incident, but I'm a man who learns from his mistakes. I make you shrimp kebabs because you like seafood and I like food on sticks. We eat on the balcony and during the Perseid meteor shower we see exactly seven shooting stars, which is an omen of good fortune. We wish on each star and our last wishes are exactly the same. "I wish to spend my life with you."

He described it all. Their first fight followed by their first make-up sex. (He kept the description to a minimum but she gave him credit for creativity. And also optimism.) The first time he took her to a college reunion and introduced her to his buddies who still called him Lefty, which she hadn't known, but which suited his two left feet perfectly. The first time they slow danced on New Year's Eve, Cooper stepping on her toes while she hummed along to "Love and Marriage." The day he took her back to the Antietam Museum where they'd had their first date. He proposed as the bugle blew for the last cavalry charge in the Civil War battle reenactment, and she said yes while the fireworks display started.

He'd imagined an entire relationship, writing each scene with a deft eye for detail and his uncanny way of knowing what would make her happy.

On the second-to-last page, he'd described their wedding. They walked down the aisle, Jorie in a lace wedding dress with a huge tulle skirt, Cooper in a top hat, her mom between them, with a hand on each of their arms, as "Ode to Joy" played. On the last page another simple heart surrounded the words, "And so on…"

Her own heart was pounding. She should say no. They didn't know each other well enough, and for most of the time they'd been dating, her mom had been dying.

Still, he'd written their fairy tale, and all she needed to do was believe.

Her tears made it hard to see the pages. When she looked up his eyes were full of the power of his story.

And so on…

Cooper didn't know how precious those words were to her. He took it for granted that they could marry each other and live happily ever after. He was offering this dream to her.

"I love you, Jorie."

"I love you, too, Cooper."

"Then marry me, already. That's how it works."

Maybe that's how it worked in his world, but it had never been that way for the Burkes.

"Don't do it for your mom, do it for us," he said. He kissed her, and she felt the same thrill she had the very first time. His shoulders were warm and strong under her hands. Here he was, and here she was, and they loved each other even if it hadn't been long enough or any of those other arguments she couldn't remember right now.

"Yes, Cooper. I'll marry you."

When they kissed again, his story got caught between them and Jorie could feel the pages against her heart.

CHAPTER ONE

Seven months later

"Mom, it's an April Fool's joke," Nadine Richford said. "No one would seriously propose this for a wedding. You totally got her, Jorie." She shook her head in admiration. Except, Jorie thought nervously, this wasn't a joke.

It was eleven-fifteen on April Fool's Day and she was meeting with Sally and Nadine Richford at one of the round ironwork tables in the lobby of the St. Renwick hotel. The fountain, whose water had doused the flames when the White House was burned by the British, was close enough that drops of spray tickled the back of her neck. Tossing pennies in the famous fountain was supposed to be good luck. Sitting in the splash zone conferred no such benefits, Jorie realized, watching as her fortunes turned as quickly and thoroughly as a wedge of Brie left on a sunny buffet table at an outdoor wedding.

The Richford wedding was the only contract

standing between her and a total collapse of her wedding planning business. Maybe she should have known better than to have such an important meeting on April Fool's Day. But Jorie had fully expected to wow the Richfords—mother and daughter—with her plans to turn the Lilac Garden and Filigree Ballroom of the St. Renwick into a fifties-themed, full-on James-Dean-*Rebel-Without-a-Cause* fantasy wedding. She was positive she'd nailed the interviews with the bride and groom-to-be, working her trademark magic to capture the essential elements of their relationship and the way they'd want to present themselves to their guests. They were supposed to love her concepts so much, they'd fall over themselves to sign on the dotted line.

Sally Richford frowned when Jorie mentioned the skinny ties and gray suits for the groomsmen. Her daughter, Nadine, giggled nervously when Jorie started to describe her idea for red-and-white accents in the flowers and linens, based on the colors of James Dean's iconic jacket and T-shirt.

"I really don't think…" Sally pushed back the gold bangle bracelets on her slender, tanned wrist.

Okay, maybe they needed a visual. Jorie pulled out the planning binder she'd put together for Nadine. During her first year in business, she'd searched long and hard to find functional but pretty binders. This style, handmade by a boutique stationer in Aspen,

was one and a half inches thick and bound in linen
in shades ranging from pale lemonade to ice-blue to
peppermint-pink. The corners were covered in white
leather, as was the spine, which was constructed so
the binder lay flat when it was opened. Jorie had yet
to meet a bride who didn't fall deeply in love with
her wedding binder. Nadine's was silvery-gray to
go with the old-time movie theme.

"In our conversations, you mentioned that you
and David went to the movies on your first date."

"The Sing-Along *Sound of Music*," Nadine said.
"David sang 'Edelweiss' to me on the way home in
the taxi."

"Doesn't everyone die at the end of *Rebel Without a Cause?*" Sally asked. She didn't sound as if
it were really a question, though. She uncrossed her
legs and stood up before Jorie could answer.

"Sal Mineo's character dies, but he's meant to be
a symbol of…" She was losing them. "That's not the
point anyway…the point is…"

Nadine clutched the strap of her purse to her
chest. The corners of her eyes were red. Brides
were always crying about something. Normally,
Jorie would have offered her a tissue, but in this
case, she didn't want to draw attention to the fact
that she'd made Nadine cry. When a bride signed the
contract, she and her mother both received a green
leather, custom-designed envelope perfectly sized

to hold a travel pack of tissues. Gloria Santana (September 2008, four hundred guests at the Widmere) had had the tissue envelope replicated as the favor for her shower guests. Tears and tissues were a big part of Jorie's business. The higher the tear count, the better.

Nadine's tears, however, were the wrong sort.

Jorie had been speaking, she realized, but now she couldn't remember what she'd been trying to say.

"Why did you think I'd want a wedding based on a movie where everyone dies?" Nadine asked. "My cousin Mira called you the wedding whisperer. Her wedding was beautiful, all springtime-in-Paris pastels and nothing about guns."

"I didn't mention guns," Jorie said. "It was just the theme, you know. Movies. We could pick a different movie. *Gone With the Wind,* maybe."

"That's a war movie!" Nadine said, turning to her mother. "What did David and I say that made her think of war? Is there something wrong with us?"

"You and David have perfectly lovely ideas," Sally said, patting her daughter's shoulder. "This isn't your fault."

"Everyone says you hire Jorie Burke because she can tell what you really want." Nadine's voice was rising now. "Does David want to shoot people?"

They had forgotten she was there. Just as well, probably.

Jorie held her smile until the Richfords disappeared through the revolving lobby doors, then she carefully closed the binder and slid it back into her black leather shoulder bag. Her brides never abandoned their wedding binders. Or cried the wrong kind of tears. Planning weddings used to be effortless. Coming up with this idea for Nadine and David had been nothing but hard work and it hadn't gotten her anywhere. She sat on the uncomfortable iron chair, splashed by the lucky fountain, and waited to see if she was going to cry. But the numbness that had settled on her when her mom died six months ago didn't seem to be affected by the impending collapse of her business.

Once she was certain she wasn't going to cry, she picked up her bag and crossed the lobby to the restroom, where she splashed water on her face and then checked her lipstick in the mirror. That was when she saw the spiky brown splotch that spread from just beneath the neckline of her gray, crepe-silk dress to the top of her left breast. It wasn't huge, but no one would miss it. She wet a paper towel, but even as she blotted the stain, she knew it was futile—the dress was ruined. She must have spilled her coffee on the way to her appointment. She'd been so preoccupied thinking about which of her outstanding bills she was going to clear with the Richfords' down payment that she hadn't even noticed. The mark had been there the entire time she'd been pitching the James Dean-themed wedding.

Two years ago, when her business had been growing faster than she could manage on her own, she'd had interns, a pair of sophisticated, romantic-minded college girls from Sweet Briar. She'd trained them to look perfect but unmemorable—brides liked their wedding planners to reflect their good taste, but they didn't like to be shown up by the help. Between the coffee stain and the fact that the wide, patent-leather belt around her waist was straining at the very last hole, she'd lost all of the image points she normally counted on during an interview. She turned sideways and ran a hand over her stomach. She'd put on weight. As much as she wished she could attribute the too-small belt to a dry cleaning accident, she knew where the blame for her expanding waistline lay. With her. Well, with her and cake. Only she and the Lord knew exactly how many slices of her friend Alice's cakes she'd consumed in the past few months. Jorie had always loved food, but since her mom died, she'd felt a desperate inability to get full, no matter how much she ate.

Chelsea Burke was probably rolling in her grave. Actually, knowing her mom, she was plotting some way to escape her grave so she could chide Jorie in person for letting herself go. Chelsea had loved to tell people, "The Burke women have always been thin." She never revealed that it wasn't genetics, but hard work, strict diets and, in her mom's case, occasional fasts, that helped maintain that image.

Jorie missed her mom. When she was little, Chelsea had moved them from city to city, searching for the next guy to support them and shelter them. They'd been a pair of chameleons, changing themselves to suit whatever guy her mom had chosen as her next possible Mr. Right. In a way it was ironic that Jorie had become a wedding planner. Building a career around the one great disappointment of her mom's life might seem twisted, but she was successful because she'd grown up with Chelsea Burke. She knew how much the idea of a wedding meant to the women who sought her out. The ones who were so desperate for the perfect day that they'd leave the planning to a stranger. She'd worked hard to make sure her brides had the wedding they'd dreamed of and she'd been successful. Until her mom died and she suddenly lost her ability to connect with anyone's wedding dreams.

She slid her lipstick into a small pocket in her leather bag and then checked that she had the binder for her next appointment, a cake tasting at Alice's bakery, where she would restrict herself to the tiniest bites possible. She may have lost her last client, but she had one more wedding to plan. She was marrying Cooper Murphy, younger brother of Senator Bailey Murphy. If her fairy-tale wedding to one of the most-desirable bachelors in Washington, D.C., couldn't put her business back on the map, she'd eat her own bouquet (blush-pink peonies, white heather and pale green hydrangea).

St. Helen's church wasn't open on weekdays. Vandalism and a skeleton staff in the parish office combined to limit the public hours. Cooper had explained to Father Chirwa that he wanted to sit in the church to write his wedding vows, and the priest had made an exception for him. If he'd been born in an earlier generation, maybe back in County Cavan before the first Murphy emigrated, they'd have said he had the gift of the gab. His brother was fond of telling people Cooper could talk Greenpeace into advocating for more whaling. Not that he would, but the potential was there.

He'd been alone in the church for two hours now. He was supposed to meet Jorie to choose their wedding cake in a little more than forty-five minutes. So far, he'd read the Stations of the Cross, lit a candle for his grandmother, said a prayer that the Nationals would find a starting pitcher and, if it wasn't too much, a center fielder who could both catch and hit. Then he'd decided that he shouldn't be praying about baseball so he'd lit another candle and prayed for peace and enlightenment and fortitude, because he'd always liked that word.

The pages of his notebook stayed stubbornly blank. He uncapped his favorite fountain pen and put a heading on the page. *Wedding Vows*. He jotted some words underneath—love, Jorie, wife, eternal and a curse word that he immediately crossed out and then apologized to God and the saints for. He took another turn around the perimeter of the church, the leather soles of his shoes making a lonely echo. When he got to the candle rack again he stopped, and this time he prayed for wisdom.

Writing the vows was his only job for the wedding and he couldn't even do that.

He slid into a pew and laid his notebook and pen down next to him. He looked at the altar; imagined himself up there, waiting for Jorie to walk down the aisle toward him. Of course, their wedding wasn't here in his home parish, but in the National Cathedral. The Wish Team, which had fulfilled Jorie's mom's wish by funding her daughter's dream wedding, had pulled strings to get the venue. Jorie was over the moon about decorating the cathedral. The exact setting didn't matter to Cooper. Soon enough, he'd be in a church, waiting for Jorie and minutes away from vowing to…something.

He leaned forward, resting his head in his hands.

The thing about marrying a wedding planner was that nothing was left to chance. Jorie had plans for every moment of the ceremony and the reception. She consulted him before making a decision because she was the kind of woman who thought men should be included in that stuff, but the wedding was really hers. Writing the vows was the only thing she'd moved permanently off her to-do list and onto his.

She said it was because he was the better writer. He'd been writing political speeches and ghostwriting op-ed pieces and thousands of other communications for close to ten years, so yeah, writing wedding vows was definitely something he should be able to do. The only trouble was…well…actually there were two problems. One, he was pretty damn sure she'd given him this job because she couldn't have done it herself. The reality was, she didn't know him, didn't really love him and hadn't ever really wanted to marry him. And number two, he was pretty sure he felt the same way.

Yeah. Those were the main issues and he had only himself to blame. It was Chelsea's idea for them to get married, and her wish, which had been expanded into a huge fundraiser for the Wish Team's tenth anniversary, was being granted even though she'd died months ago, much sooner than they'd hoped. But it had been his own inability to resist a romantic gesture that sealed the engagement.

He could have said no, but Chelsea's defiant belief in the power of wishing after a lifetime of disappointment had touched him. He'd seen the hope in her eyes that she could give Jorie this one thing before she died, and he'd said yes, because how could he not help her when he knew exactly what it meant to care that much about your family?

He and Jorie had only been dating for six months at the time and their relationship was still so new he hadn't seen any downside. He didn't stop to think about consequences, so caught up in Chelsea's dream that he couldn't have said no if he'd wanted to. His mom had been complaining about this habit of acting from the heart ever since he'd set the classroom pets loose in kindergarten. The rabbit hadn't gotten far, but two of the gerbils and the corn snake hadn't been seen again. He was the guy who always put his hand over his heart for the National Anthem. He'd given the toast at his brother's wedding and two different women had propositioned him afterward and a guy from the World Wildlife Fund had asked him to write their annual donor appeal. Which he'd done. He liked pandas as much as the next guy.

Chelsea Burke had offered him the chance to

be a knight in shining armor and he'd said yes. His fault.

His romantic impulsiveness had brought him and Jorie to this point, but his good sense had finally caught up. It was late. Too late in many ways, but they hadn't passed the irrevocable point where they pledged some as yet unwritten vows to each other. He'd screwed up and he was going to hurt a lot of people, but he'd do the right thing before it really was too late.

When he proposed to Jorie, he knew deep down that they hadn't been together long enough, didn't know each other well enough, but he'd convinced himself it wouldn't matter. If anything, he knew less about Jorie now. She was beautiful, at least to him. Her strawberry-blonde hair and sky-blue eyes meshed perfectly with creamy skin dusted with freckles. She was smart, perceptive and had a wry sense of humor he appreciated. She had impeccable fashion sense, although she tended toward the conservative, and he loved the body she kept concealed under her buttoned-up exterior.

Unfortunately, he'd found out most of those things during the first few months they were dating. Since then, he'd been unable to get closer to her. She was so guarded he couldn't find a way in. He'd become convinced that what he'd initially thought of as sophistication was actually an ingrained reserve. Or

else she didn't much like him. Either way, he was
out of ideas for how to turn his hopes for their relationship into reality.

He stood up and walked to the front of the church.
Leaning on the railing around the votive candles, he
watched the flames flicker. He put another dollar
in the metal collection box and picked up a long
wooden match, dipping it into the flame. He lit one
last candle and whispered, "I'm sorry."

He wasn't sure who the apology was for. Chelsea,
Jorie, himself? He hoped Jorie would understand.

COOPER DIDN'T KISS HER.

He had to pass her to get to his chair at Lucky's
tasting table, and he trailed one hand along the back
of her seat, grazing the skin above the collar of her
coffee-stained dress, but he didn't bend to kiss her
cheek.

Cooper always kissed her.

He kissed everyone—his mother, his brother, his
father, his many cousins, his friends. Jorie wouldn't
be surprised to find out he'd kissed his bus driver in
elementary school. A peck on the cheek in greeting
from Cooper Murphy was nothing special. Not getting one was. Especially for the woman planning to
marry him.

If she hadn't been so intent on making every
detail of her wedding perfect now that it was her

only project, she would have worried more about the missing kiss, but she had bigger fish to fry.

Red velvet fish, if all went according to plan.

Alice poked her head around the door leading to the front of the bakery. "There's our groom!" she called. "A few minutes late and Jorie had us convinced you weren't coming. Give me one second." She ducked back out of sight, the swinging door making a breeze strong enough to ruffle the edge of the cotton tablecloth.

"I didn't say you weren't coming," Jorie protested. "I'm nervous, that's all. Alice is being dramatic."

He pulled his seat out but stayed on his feet, his hands wrapped tightly around the white wooden knobs on either side of the ladder-back chair. "Listen, Jorie, I almost didn't come." He hesitated and seemed to change his mind about what to say. "I can't do this."

What was he talking about? Alice's cakes were amazing. He knew that because he'd eaten just as many pieces as she had in the past few months.

"I know you're dubious about the red velvet, but I told you, ignore the name. You're going to love it." She picked up the pale aqua menu card and tried to hand it to him. "Aren't these menus perfect? The blue and silver are our wedding colors, and see, our names and the wedding date are right here. Brides love these." Alice made individual cake menus for all of the couples who came for tastings. As keepsakes, they looked gorgeous mounted in Jorie's wedding binders.

He took the menu but didn't read it. "I was working on the vows all morning."

The vows. She was almost afraid to ask what he'd written. Elise Gordon (348 guests, silver and white New Year's wedding) had written rhyming vows which her husband rapped to her. (The rhymes had been planned; the rap was spur of the moment.) Jorie wasn't interested in a rap, but she did wonder what Cooper would promise and what he'd ask from her in return. Her mom had never gotten any of her boyfriends to the vow stage, and it had seemed to Jorie that her mom had consistently given more than she got.

Alice backed through the door just then, a tray held in front of her. "I am so sorry, guys. The counter is crazy busy and my full-time help is home with a sick kid." She slid the silver tray holding four small cakes onto the table. "I'd love to give you the full treatment, but I'm going to have to leave you on your own." She pointed to the cake at the top of the tray. "This is the carrot. Start here." She pointed at each one, moving clockwise around the grouping. "Carrot. Lemon. Red velvet. Chocolate. Small bites. Taste each one before you make up your mind. The usual drill, Jorie. Don't let your man taste out of order—he'll ruin the flavors."

She beamed at them. "Of all the weddings we're doing this year, yours is going to be the most perfect." Her eyes sparkled under the brim of her Lucky's ball cap. "Your mom would have loved this."

The bell rang in the front of the bakery and Alice put two forks and a serving spatula next to the china dessert plates on the table. "Enjoy!" She rushed back through the door, leaving them alone.

The tasting room at Lucky's was tucked behind the actual store. Alice had told her she'd picked grass-green for the walls with white accents because bright spaces made people hungry. Cooper, standing behind his chair, didn't seem to be falling under the spell. Jorie leaned back so she could see him better. His thick brown hair, dark chocolate eyes and deep dimples were such a perfect combination, they still made her tingle, but she couldn't read his expression. Cooper was characteristically open and uncomplicated. It was one of the reasons she'd been attracted to him. But today, he wouldn't meet her eye. He still hadn't sat down.

And he hadn't kissed her.

She turned the tray a fraction so that the carrot cake was positioned at exactly twelve o'clock. She was reading too much into that missing kiss. He'd been late and he was distracted. She was upset about losing Nadine's wedding. *So what if he hadn't kissed her?* It didn't mean anything. It certainly didn't mean...

He put the menu on the table, so close to the tray that the top corner made a divot in the icing on the carrot cake. She'd have to ask Alice for an extra copy; that stained one might ruin her binder.

"Jorie," he said, and his voice was soft. He had a terrific voice, rich and rumbly, but it could be incredibly gentle. "I wanted this to work out, you know I did. But I can't...I couldn't write the vows." He looked away, his glance bouncing around the room, which was decorated with oversize black and white prints of brides and grooms. "We have to call it off."

He wasn't doing this. He wouldn't. She wouldn't let him. Her stomach was starting to hurt and she really wanted to take off her belt.

"Please sit down," she said. "You're too tall and I'm never going to be able to cut even slices with you looming over me."

She pushed his chair out with her foot, a little harder than necessary. He stepped back quickly to avoid getting hit in the gut, and she panicked. He was leaving.

"You have to sit down!" she said and he did. She picked up the cake server. "Carrot first."

He covered her hand with his own. "Please stop talking about cake."

"Why? Why can't we get this done? Why can't one thing go right today?" She pulled her hand away from his. "My belt is too small, my dress is stained and I lost the Richford contract this morning because all of my ideas are stupid. Is it so awful that I'd like to sit here in Alice's pretty room and eat these cakes with you?"

"You lost the Richford contract?" He shifted slightly toward her. "I'm sorry."

For the first time, he looked straight at her. She'd always thought those deep brown eyes gave him an unfair advantage. Cooper was a truly good guy, kind, honest, romantic. He looked so trustworthy, she didn't know how anyone could ever doubt him.

"They didn't love my *Rebel Without a Cause* theme."

"Everyone dies at the end of that movie."

"Sal Mineo dies. Everyone else is fine."

"That other kid dies in the chicken scene."

"He was a bully!"

"Still, not exactly the first film you think of for a wedding."

Jorie pulled the tray closer and cut a thick wedge of the red velvet. She wasn't going to agree to lemon or carrot, so why mess around? "Maybe you shoul have come to the meeting. You seem to have the same taste in weddings as Sally and Nadine." She flipped the slice onto his plate and speared a bite with his fork. She held it up and he hesitated, then took it. His mouth curved around the fork. Cooper had a beautiful mouth with strong, sculpted lips.

"That's delicious."

"See? I know what I'm talking about. I knew you'd love that one."

"Liking the same cake doesn't mean we should get married."

"What?" The desperate, deliberate innocence in her voice reminded her so much of her mom that she could almost see Chelsea sitting at the table with them. How many times had her mom tried to hold on to a guy who was letting her down easy? How often had Jorie promised herself she'd never be that begging woman?

He folded his hands, pressing them together.

"It's what I've been trying to tell you. Badly. I want to call off the wedding. If we go through with it, we'll be lying. To my family, to our friends. To each other."

"I'm not lying," she whispered. She laid the fork gently down on the edge of his plate. She put her hand on his wrist, wanting to hold onto him and hating herself for wanting it.

"We are, Jorie. I tried to write the vows and I

couldn't. I kept winding up back at your mom. We're doing this for her." He shook his head. "We don't even know each other."

"I knew you'd like red velvet cake."

"That's not enough."

"Of course it's not." She dropped his wrist. She knew as well as anyone that cake wasn't enough. "Why is this suddenly coming up now? When you proposed, I said no. Remember? I said it was too soon and my mom was wedding-crazed as usual. But you persuaded me. You said we had a great start and we could build on it and we should give my mom this last gift because what better way to start a life together?" She slid out of her chair and walked a few steps before turning back. "You had your big romantic moment. You wrote me a fairy tale. And now I've got everything wrapped up in this wedding—my business, my reputation, the fundraiser for my mom's registry, everything! And you're going to leave me hanging?"

He poked the tines of his fork into the icing on the edge of the plate.

"I never meant to hurt you."

"What *did* you mean, then? You asked me to marry you. Isn't that what you wanted?"

"I wanted to make your mom happy. To make you happy. I thought it would all work out."

She stared at him. "No wonder," she said. "You're

a romantic just like her. Things don't 'work out.' You have to work at them. You have to try."

"We have tried."

"No, we haven't," she said quickly. "We've been tiptoeing around each other ever since my mom died."

The fork clattered on the plate. He shook his head and pushed his chair back, not making eye contact. "I'm sorry. Jorie, you're a great person. I wanted your mom to be happy and I wanted you to be happy, but I can't marry you. It will only make more problems."

He was walking out. Just like that. He'd decided things were over and it didn't matter what she said or what she wanted.

"We have to at least try," she whispered. "I can't—" *become my mother* "—ruin my mother's last wish."

"Your mom is the reason we got engaged. I can't get married for her, too."

She didn't know what to say. Her life was ending right here at the tasting table in the back room at Lucky's. Her engagement. Her chance at being the woman Cooper Murphy chose to marry. The moment when she proved once and for all that she wasn't going to live her mother's life.

He leaned down and she hoped he'd changed his mind. Maybe he was going to kiss her and everything else he'd said would fade into a bad dream. "I'm so sorry that I hurt you," he said, very quietly.

She couldn't speak. He didn't kiss her. The door closed behind him and she was alone with her tray of untasted cakes and two dirty forks.

COOPER PAUSED AFTER HE closed the door. *Nice going, jackass.* He'd handled that about as badly as possible. He'd been screwing this up right from the start and it had ended with Jorie getting hurt. He rubbed his wrist, pressing the spot where she'd held him tightly. Jorie didn't cling. She didn't beg. Hell, she hardly ever asked. He was hard pressed to remember an instance in the time he'd known her when she'd asked him for something that didn't have to do with the wedding.

He shook his head. That was the point. She didn't want anything from him. He and Jorie didn't have a relationship, they had plans for a wedding.

As he passed the big front window of the bakery, he glimpsed Alice through the glass. Her mouth opened when she saw him, and she glanced over her shoulder toward the tasting room. Good. Jorie wouldn't be alone. He was halfway across the street, heading toward his office, hoping he could finally make some progress on the speech he was supposed to be writing for his brother, when his phone rang. He checked the caller ID. "Dad?"

"We need you at the house."

"What's wrong?" A list went through his mind... Mom, Bailey, Dad. Was someone sick? "Dad, what's happened? Is Mom...?"

"Your mother is fine. How long before you can get here?"

"I..." He shifted the phone to his left hand and glanced at his watch. "Fifteen minutes? Why?"

"I don't want to talk on the cell. I'll tell you when you get here."

So it was politics. Something was up with Bailey.

"Are you sure you need me?" he asked. "Because Jorie and I—"

"Make it ten if you can," his dad said, and then he hung up.

Good old Dad. Whenever the tension went up, his carefully cultivated interpersonal skills went out the window, and he turned into the predator Nolan Murphy, driven, focused, ruthless when necessary. If he weren't so brilliant, Cooper thought, it would be easy to dislike the guy. As it was, if his dad said jump, Cooper asked how high and never stopped to question why jumping was required.

CHAPTER TWO

ALICE PUSHED OPEN THE door to the tasting room. "Did Cooper leave?"

"He liked the red velvet," Jorie said. She thought she'd done a good job of sounding exactly like a bride-to-be after a satisfactory cake tasting, but when Alice came all the way into the room and crouched down next to the table, she knew she'd failed.

"What happened?"

"He didn't think he was going to like it." Jorie used two fingers to slide the silver tray away from her. The uneaten cakes were making her nauseous and she thought vomiting in Alice's tasting room might be bad for their friendship. "Whoever named it should have done better market research because that sucker is a tough sell. Velvet is fuzzy, you know?"

Alice didn't respond.

"He called off the engagement."

Saying it out loud made it real. Alice sat back on her heels, apparently at a loss for words. She was only the first, Jorie realized. Everyone she told would look at her with exactly the same shock mixed with pity. She'd have to notify the caterers and the hotel. She'd need to call the priest and cancel the church, but first, she'd have to call the Wish Team. They'd pulled strings to get the National Cathedral. That call would be the cap on the dissolution of her life. Once the wedding was canceled, this whole dream would be down the drain. She'd be her mother, trying to cobble some new life together after she'd lost her latest man. There was no way she'd be able to pull her business back from the brink after this. Who would hire the wedding planner who couldn't even drag her own man to the altar?

No.

She wasn't going to watch her life fall apart. She regretted saying anything to Alice.

"I don't think he meant it, though," she said quickly. "He said he was working on the vows. It could have been cold feet."

"Tell me what he said."

The door to the bakery opened and the college boy who was working the register stuck his head into the room. "Sorry to interrupt, Alice, but there's a woman here who says she ordered five dozen coconut cupcakes and the only ones in the cooler are strawberry cheesecake."

"They're on the top shelf, already boxed. Find them. I'm with a bride."

"Not exactly," Jorie muttered.

The door closed again and Alice pulled the empty chair around and sat down, facing Jorie. "I want to hear what happened."

"You have customers."

"They can wait. Tell me."

"He said he can't marry me," Jorie whispered. She should get up and leave before she embarrassed herself any more, but she didn't.

The door swung open again. "Alice, what's the register code for the apple pie?"

"Pies are free for the next fifteen minutes. Tell the customers it's a cooked fruit freebie frenzy." Alice narrowed her eyes at her assistant. "Also, Eliot? You go to Georgetown. You can manage the bakery by yourself for five minutes. It's straightforward. Take in dollars. Hand over carbohydrates."

Eliot retreated.

"I'm so sorry about that," Alice said.

"You know what? I shouldn't be surprised. I'm not the easiest person to love. I'm private and prickly and I've never been good at relationships." Jorie paused. She could hear her voice rising and she really didn't want to lose control. She and Alice were friends, but not the kind who bared their souls—it was bad enough she couldn't seem to stop talking.

"But I thought Cooper knew me. I thought he was okay with me."

Alice put her hands on Jorie's shoulders. "I'll give you private, but I don't see prickly. Whatever Cooper's problem is, it's not you."

Jorie looked down at the table.

"Right?" Alice prompted.

"Sure." Jorie sighed. "Do you think we'll have to give the Wish Registry gifts back?" When she and Cooper had agreed they didn't want gifts for their wedding, her mom had been disappointed that she wouldn't get to help Jorie fill out the registry. It had been Chelsea's inspiration, so typical of her generous spirit, that had led to the Wish Registry. It included everything from music lessons to sports tickets to trips and video game systems—a list of wishes the foundation had matched with recipients. Her mom had insisted that they wrap each item, even if it was only a gift certificate or trip itinerary, so the recipient would have something tangible. "My mom loved that stupid registry so much."

"And you love Cooper, right?" Alice asked gently. "You were marrying him because you love him, not for your mom, right?"

"How could I not love Cooper?" she asked.

Alice let that go. "Are you too prickly for a hug?" Any other day Jorie would have felt like an idiot for being so publicly distressed, but today seemed to be a day of firsts. When Alice pulled her in and hugged her, she closed her eyes and leaned into the contact. She did love Cooper. Or she would have loved Cooper once they were married. She was quite sure she had the right feelings about him. She liked his company. They had good talks. She liked the way he looked. They were great in bed. She'd talked to enough couples to know that she wasn't exactly passionately in love, but she was close. If only she had a little more time.

COOPER TOOK THE FRONT steps to the Georgetown row house he'd grown up in two at a time. On the way there, he'd imagined about fifty really bad reasons his dad wanted to meet him at home in the middle of the day. It was probably politics, but Cooper, who spent his life writing inspiring speeches, had a very good imagination.

His mom opened the door when he knocked, and because she'd been on his list of possible casualties, he gave her a hug in addition to his usual kiss on the cheek. His dad had told him she was fine, but his dad had lied to him before. Of course, Nolan Murphy would call it keeping him on a need-to-know basis. His dad's standards were far from black and white when it came to the truth.

"Good to see you, Mom," he said. "You look great." She did, too. Rachel Murphy was tall, blonde and fit. She also had one of the best policy minds on the East Coast. She played up her feminine side with color and flowing fabrics and bold jewelry. She said her décolletage had bamboozled more senators into more deals than half the lobbying firms in the city. When he patted her shoulder, he was relieved to feel the familiar taut muscles earned from a lifetime of tennis. "Nice and healthy."

Rachel hugged him back and then straightened, one hand still on his forearm. "Your dad didn't fill you in on what's going on, did he? He let you worry?"

He nodded.

"I'm telling you, Cooper. That man knows better than to torment you. The short answer is, it's your brother. Bailey has gotten himself into a serious mess and I don't see a way out for him this time. Your dad and Theo are still working out the angles, but I think it's going to mean resignation—your dad just hasn't come to grips with that yet."

"Resignation" sent a jolt through him. A Murphy was going to resign from his Senate seat? What the hell could Bailey have done? His mom and dad lived and breathed the Senate—they had since long before Cooper was born. His mom had married into the family, but she seemed just as proud as his dad to remind people there'd been a Murphy in the Senate since 1968.

"Resign, Mom? What happened?"

"It's not something that happened. It's something he did. Deliberately and without even considering what it would mean for us. For your father. For his committees. For the votes he has coming up. For anyone."

She was past furious. Usually the family could count on her to be the voice of reason. Not this time.

"You coming in?" he asked her.

"I've given them my opinion already, and frankly, I shouldn't be around Bailey right now. I would hate for this situation to get any more acrimonious than it already is, but he has really...the idea that someone with his gifts would flush it all—" Rachel patted Cooper's arm, her face tight with controlled anger. "It's better for everyone if I stay out of the way for a while."

"But..." Cooper didn't know what to say. His entire life, his mom and dad had been the team in charge of the Murphys' political fortunes. Other families had holiday traditions, annual vacations or shared religion to keep them together. The Murphys had politics. "Don't you need to—"

"The thing I *don't* need is to see your brother right now."

Your brother. That's what she used to call Bailey when he was in high school and had taken some stupid risk or failed to excel in class. At least she hadn't called him "your goddamn brother." That was more their dad's thing.

"Okay. Well. I'll go in and see what Dad wants."

She patted his arm again, this time with a tight smile. "You're going to do fine."

And that absolutely unreassuring little statement sent his tension soaring.

He was halfway down the hall, a few steps past the dark walnut pocket doors that opened onto the formal living room, when she called after him. "I forgot to ask, did you pick a cake?"

He closed his eyes for half a second but didn't turn around. "The red velvet was good."

His mom laughed. "Jorie was right, huh? You'd think you'd trust the wedding planner even if you don't trust your bride."

He was going to hate telling her about the wedding. He'd never liked disappointing his mom. As far back as elementary school when he'd rush home to show her his report card, he'd wanted her to be proud of him. It hadn't always been easy for him. Bailey was the golden boy who'd been marked as their father's political heir sometime in the few seconds between clearing the birth canal and having the doctor count all his fingers and toes. Other than ending up two inches taller, Cooper had never done anything as well as his brother. If you compared their driver's licenses, even the height difference was erased because Bailey shared their father's more flexible approach to the truth.

Which was probably part of the reason for this meeting. Whatever was going on was bad. Bad enough that his mom wasn't even speaking to Bailey.

WHEN HE PUSHED THE DOOR to the study open, the first thing Cooper noticed was that his brother was standing on the far side of the room, leaning on the low table in front of the window, his back to the other two men. His dad and his cousin Theo were seated together all the way on the opposite side of the room at the library table near the fireplace, notebooks and laptops open, cell phones at their elbows, heads close together as they talked.

Holy crap. Bailey was already out.

He didn't care what his mom had said about no decisions having been made. It was one hundred percent clear that his dad and Theo were working on a problem and Bailey...across the room by himself...Bailey *was* that problem. Cooper let his palm rest flat on the heavy swinging door for a moment, the weight of the wood grounding him. He'd grown up knowing his brother was the center of the family universe and now, without warning, Bailey was sidelined. He didn't know if he should go to his brother or join his dad and cousin. Nothing about this situation was normal.

"Cooper," his dad said. "Take a seat. We've got a lot to cover."

Bailey didn't move, still hadn't looked at him, but his voice was bitter as he said, "You shouldn't do this to him. Saint Cooper doesn't know how to say no to you."

"I'm not the one causing problems," Nolan said. "Cooper will do what needs to be done. What's right for the family. He understands what's expected of him. He's not the one who's been carrying on behind his wife's back with an investment banker who's going to give birth to his illegitimate child smack in the middle of his reelection campaign!" He practically shouted the last words.

So much for having a lot to cover, Cooper thought. Senator Bailey Murphy of Pennsylvania, married to one woman and having a baby with another. Not much more to explain, was there?

Nolan pointed at the chair next to him. "Let's go, Cooper. We need you now."

He stepped into the room, letting the door swish closed behind him, but he didn't sit down. Bailey still hadn't turned around. Cooper had grown up worshipping Bailey. He was the kind of magnetic, larger-than-life guy a little brother either hated or idolized. He didn't inspire moderate reactions in anyone. Even his election had been a landslide, but then, the voters of Pennsylvania had been making a statement about more than the telegenic, charismatic Murphy heir. Their dad had resigned his seat when he'd been tapped as a vice-presidential nominee. It had been an enormous coup, but marked the end of his career when his ticket got crushed in the election. He'd thrown his weight behind Bailey as the Senate candidate in the special election to fill his seat, and the voters of Pennsylvania turned out to honor him by electing his son.

Working with and for Bailey the past six years had deepened his relationship with his brother, but Cooper didn't exactly worship him anymore. He still loved him. He admired him, and more than anything else, he knew him. Bailey was in pain. The way he'd lashed out now meant that whatever he'd done, it hadn't been a whim. His brother was serious.

"Well, since I'm not married, it stands to reason I couldn't mess around with anyone, much less an investment banker, behind my wife's back," Cooper said. "Besides, I've never been a money guy."

"See?" the bitterness was still in Bailey's voice. "I told you to leave him out of this—he doesn't want to be involved."

"And I told you to shut up about two hours ago," Nolan said. "Try to see if you can do a better job keeping your mouth zipped than you did with your pants."

Cooper winced, but he could hear the hurt in his father's tone. His dad swore he only had high expectations for Bailey because he was capable of meeting them. Nothing made him angrier than the thought that Bailey was throwing away opportunities.

Theo tapped his pen on the table. "Whoa, guys, we agreed sniping at each other wasn't productive." He was wearing jeans and a hoodie from Georgetown and his Steelers cap was turned backward, but he still managed to sound like the three-hundred-dollar-an-hour lawyer he was. "Let's get Cooper up to speed and then we'll see where to go next. The clock is ticking—the more time we waste, the bigger chance we have of losing our one shot at spinning this our way."

When he finished, Nolan was still glaring at Bailey's back as if he hadn't even spoken. Theo gave Cooper a "please help me" look. Cooper liked his cousin. Theo was supersmart and he had a wicked sense of humor. It made him a sought-after speaker and an excellent storyteller at the bar after a few glasses of Scotch. Not that he told stories about his family, but there were always tales to be told about somebody in Washington.

Theo thought Cooper was a soft touch—hell, everyone in his family thought he was. But he respected Cooper's opinion. He pushed a chair out from the table with his foot and Cooper hesitated before sitting down. He didn't want to be there, but this was his family. He'd do what he had to to help them out.

"Should I ask Mom to come in before we start?"

"Mom's not talking to me," Bailey muttered. "If she comes in, you have to promise you'll check her for weapons."

"Enough!" Nolan said.

It took twenty minutes for Theo to lay it all out for Cooper. There were details he wished he could unlearn. The woman with the baby wasn't interested in publicity, but she wasn't going to go away either. The baby was undeniably Bailey's. Those were the main points. Bailey was going to be a dad—Cooper couldn't take that in. He had to stop himself from interrupting because he kept thinking Theo was skipping something important, something that he couldn't quite grasp. As his cousin went through the recap, the weight of the debacle settled on him.

And it was a debacle. Bailey was done. *God.* His brother had all the gifts in the world. He could have been a legend. Except he was still human—still the same guy Cooper had grown up with, brilliant but unpredictable.

"So, Cooper." His dad leaned toward him, the intensity in his brown eyes as unnerving as it had been when Cooper was a kid and committed some transgression. "We need you to write the speech of a lifetime. When Bailey reads the speech, it has to convince the people of Pennsylvania, and most of all, Governor Karloski, that your brother has made one, small, forgivable mistake. That his loving wife, Jill, is sticking with him in this troubled time, that he is deeply, truly sorry for said small error, and that, with the best interests of Pennsylvania in mind, he has made the difficult, but honorable decision to step down." He counted off each point, tapping a thick finger on the legal pad in front of him. "And most importantly, you need to lay the subtle kernel of a notion that the very best person to pick up the end of Bailey's term is his devoted and deserving brother. That's the linchpin, Coop. We need you in there now."

There was so much that was wrong with what his dad had just said. For one thing, according to Theo, Jill was currently on her way to her mom's house in the Poconos with a divorce lawyer already on speed dial. Cooper wasn't stupid, but it really did take him a second for the most important thing his dad had said to sink in. "Me? You want me to run for the Senate?"

Theo pushed his notebook toward Cooper. He'd sketched what looked like a timeline and now he ticked off each point with his pen. "You're not running for anything. Bailey resigns and the governor appoints someone to finish his term. That's you. Because the primary is already over, the state party committee is allowed to select the candidate to run in the general election. That's me. I win the seat and you're off the hook by next January."

"Why aren't you taking the seat right now?" It had long been understood that if anything happened to Bailey, Theo was the designated heir.

"Too young."

Cooper looked at his dad.

"He can't be sworn in until he's thirty, which he won't be until October," Nolan said. "If any of this had been planned, we could have worked the timing and made sure Theo was ready. But your goddamn brother hasn't left us any wiggle room and Theo is not a viable option at the moment. Which is why we need you."

Bailey hadn't turned around. Hadn't opened his mouth since their dad told him to shut up. Cooper realized what had been missing from the facts as they were laid out.

"I need to talk to Bailey," he said. "Alone."

"Later," his dad said. "If we don't get in front of this thing today, we can kiss the seat goodbye. Karloski is going to have to sell you to a lot of unhappy people. We need to give him every inch of help we can. Your uncle Stephen is on his way to Harrisburg right now."

Cooper stood up. He'd never been comfortable with defiance. Ever since he was a kid he'd been able to talk his way out of difficult situations without confrontation. But this issue was black-and-white and had to be met head-on.

"Dad, you're talking about this as if it's a done deal. I've never run for anything in my—"

His dad interrupted, chopping the air with an impatient swipe. "You're not running now. You're being appointed. We're taking care of it. But it won't happen if you don't sit the hell down and let us get started."

"I won't be long." Cooper walked toward the door.

"You're wasting time we don't have," his dad said.

He pushed the door open. His neck prickled as if his dad's stare was a living thing, ready to leap on him. He owed his brother the chance to explain. He didn't check to see if Bailey was coming. He didn't need to. He heard a loud smack and guessed his dad had hit the table. In the kitchen he pulled out two beers and used the bottle opener mounted on the edge of the stainless-steel-covered island to open them. He took a long swallow from one bottle and held the other one out just as Bailey came through the door. The beer ran cold down his throat but did nothing to settle his thoughts, which were pretty much an infinite loop of "Senator Cooper Murphy" and "holy hell" and "out of their freaking minds."

"Drinking on the job already, Cooper?"

"Don't," he said.

"Don't what?" Bailey took a pull of his own beer, but he flicked a glance sideways at Cooper.

"Don't be flip. Don't pretend you're an asshole. I'm not Dad."

Bailey nodded and put his beer down on the island. Cooper leaned forward, exhausted by what was turning out to be an incredibly long and horrible day.

"What do you want to know?"

"You're too smart for this to have been a mistake or a surprise. You got her pregnant on purpose. If you wanted out, why not just withdraw from the campaign?"

Bailey glanced toward the closed door and then sighed. "I don't know why Dad never believes me when I tell him you're the devious one."

"I can't believe you'd do this. Not to your staff or the family. Jill. What the hell, Bay? Why not just retire?"

"Because they wouldn't have let me."

Cooper started to protest but Bailey stopped him.

"Don't pretend it's not true. I could never stand

up to them. You were in there—Dad and Uncle
Stephen, Mom, even Theo—they're relentless. Be-
sides, it's not just the job, Coop. It's my life. Bailey
Murphy. I hate freaking Bailey Murphy. If Jill and
I were ever in love, that ended years ago. In the
past couple years, we haven't even been friends."
He leaned back on the counter. "She's having an
affair with Cal Dobbs."

Cooper winced. He'd heard rumors, seen some
things that didn't add up, but he'd always thought Jill
had better taste. Cal had a bad haircut and a worse
personality. And he cheated at golf. Among other
things, apparently.

"I used to get a charge out of the job, but that's
not enough. I want a whole life. I want to be with
someone I can love and do something I care about
because it's mine, not because someone decided it
should be mine for no reason other than that I was
born first. I met Deb and…she's what I want. Her
and the baby. As long as I was Senator Murphy, I
couldn't be with her. I couldn't see another way
out."

"Divorce?"

Bailey shook his head.

He was right. Divorce would have gotten him out
of the marriage, but he wanted out of the job, too.
Out of his life.

"You could have thrown a debate. Messed up a speech."

"No one cares about that stuff except guys like you. It wouldn't have affected the election."

Cooper crossed to the round wooden breakfast table in a windowed nook overlooking the backyard. He sat, putting his beer next to him, stretching his legs in front of him, wishing he could figure out what he was supposed to feel. Growing up, he and Bailey had eaten dinner at this table more often than not. When their parents were both home, the family ate in the dining room, but nights when all four of them were around at the same time had been rare. He'd been close to Bailey and he knew his brother had struggled with their parents' expectations when he was younger, but he'd seemed to grow out of that. Maybe he'd just gotten better at hiding it.

He wasn't sure what he was going to say to his dad, but he was certain of one thing.

"I'm not taking this unless you swear to me you want out. If they're pushing you out or there's something else going on, you tell me now and we'll deal with it together."

"You'd stand up for me against Dad?" Bailey asked.

"Say the word."

"I want out," Bailey said.

Cooper pushed himself up. "That's it then." When he passed his brother, Bailey grabbed his arm.

"If you'd stand up to him for me, Coop, you should do it for yourself, too. Don't let them ram this down your throat."

"I'm not—"

"You go back in there and they won't give you any time to think. You're going to be handing your life over to them because you know and I know that the Murphy legacy has always meant more to Dad and Uncle Stephen, to all of them, than any one of us. Ever since he lost the vice presidency, it's gotten worse. Even Mom is obsessed."

Cooper blinked at the intensity on Bailey's face.

"If I don't take it, what happens?"

Bailey shrugged. "They went over all that before you got here. If they can't get you in, they're going with Harry Small—he's a D.A. in Pittsburgh. The trouble is, he'll want to run for the seat and Dad thinks he'd have a better than decent chance of getting the committee to back him for the nomination."

"So Theo wouldn't run. No more Murphys in the Senate."

"That wouldn't be the worst thing, Coop. It's not your problem."

"For you and me, maybe it's not the end of the

world. But for the rest of them…they'd never forgive you."

"I'm not sure they're going to forgive me anyway." Bailey took another swig of beer. "Mom's seriously not talking to me. She said something about polluting Dad's legacy and then she walked out."

"They'll forgive you." It would take time, but they'd come around. Cooper didn't want to think about what his brother must be feeling right now. Politics wasn't just their family business. In a lot of ways, it *was* their family. "Although if we lose the seat because of this, I doubt Uncle Stephen would ever talk to you again." He deliberately singled out their uncle, but they both knew he'd left their dad's name unspoken. Before today Cooper wouldn't have thought his mom would go that far, but now he wasn't so sure. "You're having a kid, Bay. Now isn't the time to lose your family."

That was probably when it sank in that Bailey had jumped ship. He'd met someone named Deb, fallen in love with her, and had a baby on the way. He'd risked everything to give himself a chance at the life he wanted, but he wouldn't be totally happy without the family. No matter what doubts he had about taking Bailey's seat, Cooper wouldn't say no. Not if it meant the seat stayed in Murphy hands long enough for Theo to get elected. That would leave the door open and Bailey might be able to salvage a relationship with their parents.

Bailey glanced away. "I want you to meet Deb," he said. "I think you're going to like her. She reminds me a little of Jorie."

Cooper patted his brother's shoulder. For the second time, he found himself unable to tell a member of his family that he'd ended his engagement. "I'd like to meet her." He hesitated, not sure what else to say. "I want you to be happy." That was true. He'd always wanted that. He just hadn't known how far from happy his brother was.

"Thanks."

"A baby, man." He pulled Bailey in and hugged him hard. "Congratulations."

When he stepped back, Bailey was grinning—the same grin that had probably won him a few thousand votes all on its own. "Thanks, Coop. You're the first one to say that."

COOPER WENT BACK TO the study by himself. He'd have to get used to this, he guessed. Starting today, he was going to be standing on his own, without Bailey in front of him. That made two losses for the day—his brother and Jorie. He missed them both.

He pushed the study door open. "I'll do it," he announced.

"Thank God I have one son left with some sense."

His dad stood and shook his hand. Cooper didn't know what to feel. He'd never wanted this, still didn't really want it. He'd spent his entire life being Bailey's younger brother. That role was comfortable. He knew his strengths—writing speeches was one of them—but put him in front of a crowd and ask him to deliver the words on his own? No way. He could do it, but he hated it. He hoped this temporary appointee gig wouldn't include many public speaking obligations.

"We're going to need to get Jorie over here to brief her. Give Theo her number and he can call her." Nolan sat back down. "Good thing Theo is one of your groomsmen. We can use the press coverage of the wedding to our advantage."

"Uh, Dad," he said. "I broke off the engagement."

His dad pushed his chair back and stood so fast it tipped over. "What the hell are you talking about?"

"I broke off the engagement. Right before you called me."

"My God! You and your brother are going to ruin this family. How could you be so stupid?"

"It didn't have anything to do with the family, Dad."

"You don't think Cheating Senator's Brother Breaks Heart of Grieving Fiancée is going to be a story that gets picked up? Or did you forget somehow that your wedding is the kickoff event for the tenth anniversary of the Wish Team, a group that grants goddamn wishes to people who are dying? How is the governor supposed to appoint you if you're no better than your brother?"

"When I broke up with her, I had no idea Bailey was resigning," Cooper said. "Maybe it's a good thing—I won't be distracted by the wedding. Total focus for the new job."

He looked to his cousin for support, but Theo said, "There's no way, Coop. You're going to get crucified. Bailey made sure of that."

"Get her back," his dad said flatly.

"You can't honestly expect me to marry Jorie because you say so."

His dad clenched his fists.

Theo spoke up. "What did Jorie say?"

"What?"

"Is she happy? Did she agree?"

Cooper remembered the bleak look on her face. "No."

His dad nodded eagerly. "That's good then. Right." He turned to Theo and continued speaking as if Cooper wasn't in the room. "So we'll have him tell her he changed his mind. He can get her back and no one will be the wiser."

"No one except me! You can't be serious."

"You don't have to marry her. Postpone the wedding until after the election and then you can break up again."

"Dad, listen to yourself. I'm not doing that to her."

"If you dump her now," Theo said, "your breakup is going to be dragged into Bailey's screwed-up situation which will kill her business. Who's going to hire a wedding planner whose own wedding turned into such a public circus? No bride will want to think about an affair and a broken engagement every time she gets advice from Jorie. Go to her and explain. Buy some time for both of you so she can get out of this with her dignity intact."

Cooper didn't like the way his dad looked so delighted with this solution. On the other hand, Jorie had been hurt enough. Theo's issue with her business aside, having their breakup splashed all over the news would heap more hurt on her. She'd already had an awful year, losing her mom with so little warning. He didn't want to marry her, but he didn't wish her any more sadness. He owed it to her to give her the choice.

"I'll talk to her."

"And then you'll get right back here because we're already behind," his dad said.

"I'll talk to Jorie and then come back here," he agreed.

"Tell her we'll need to brief her. I'll set up an appointment and have someone call her."

It was already starting. The switch from a private, ordinary life to a very public one. His dad wouldn't be calling Jorie to make a casual lunch date the way a regular father-in-law would. Instead she'd be squeezed in, reminders would be sent, and his dad's BlackBerry would beep exactly seven minutes before the meeting. Jorie had gone from fiancée to business asset in one afternoon.

He didn't see his mom or Bailey when he was leaving the house. Outside on the sidewalk, he thought about calling a cab. It was getting dark and he couldn't remember the last time he'd eaten. He'd had a bite of cake at Alice's, but before that maybe coffee he'd bought on the way to the church? He decided to walk. He could grab something to eat and get his thoughts together on the way.

He pulled out the small, leather-bound notebook he carried. He got some of his best ideas while he was walking and he was going to need all of his skill tonight. Somehow, between here and Jorie's house, he had to figure out how the hell to tell her that his brother had messed things up for all of them.

He flipped the notebook open, looking for a blank page. He paused at the place where he'd tried to write his wedding vows, looking at the few words he'd managed, feeling sick about what his dad had asked him to do.

If she'd agree to postpone their breakup for a few months, he'd help her plan how to back out gracefully. At least he'd have a chance to smooth over his fumbling breakup that afternoon.

Flipping the page, he wrote *1. Bailey. 2. Senate.* He hesitated, his pen resting on the notebook. What next? He scribbled *3. Me + You (for now).* Which worked fine as a subject heading, but the content? What was he going to tell her exactly? That they'd have to pretend to be in love for a few more months? That was it, right?

Great. He closed the book. Now all he had to do was fill in the details that would persuade Jorie. No sweat.

CHAPTER THREE

WHEN SHE GOT home, Jorie wanted to be depressed. She would spend her days doing nothing but watching daytime TV in her rattiest sweats while eating chocolate and processed cheese products. It was something jilted brides and the recently unemployed should do. It was what she'd never done. She'd spent so many years working hard to build her business and her life, to prove that she wasn't going to be like her mom, wouldn't have to wait for a man to complete her, and now, here she was anyway. Jilted and left with nothing. Depression was the obvious next step. She'd bought the Cheetos on the way home, and now all she needed was the sweats.

She dropped the coffee-stained dress on her bedroom floor and stepped on it deliberately. The heels she'd abandoned by the foot of the bed and the dress were the only things out of place in the room. That was going to change. She was pretty sure she would become messy during her depression.

Deep in the bottom drawer of her cherry dresser, she found the T-shirt she'd bought at the Dirty Bird

Bar when she went to Ocean City for spring break back in college. The fabric was so worn it was threadbare. That shirt, together with a pair of sweats she'd stolen from a boyfriend years ago, gave her the perfect outfit for her new lifestyle.

She sat on the bed to put the sweats on, then picked up her shoes. She stopped herself just as she was about to place them on the rack in her closet. Neatness was a habit, after all. One she could break. She let the heels fall back to the floor, and when one of them landed inside the closet accidentally, she gave it a kick to the middle of the room.

She stuck with the depression plan through one small bowl of Cheetos and three do-it-yourself shows with borderline attractive hosts. Her fingers turned orange. She missed the real butter and eggs in Alice's cakes.

She thought about Cooper saying she was lying, and anger flared, spoiling her depression.

Maybe she should turn on her computer and order some pajama bottoms because her ratty sweats weren't presentable enough to wear if she had to run to the corner store. But she really shouldn't waste the money. Who knew how long she'd have to make her savings last.

She glanced across the room at the top drawer of the sideboard where she'd locked up her inheritance from her mom. Some people might think of the

jewelry as a safety net, but Jorie had sworn she'd
never use it, no matter how broke she was. When
she'd made that promise, her business hadn't been
down the tubes, but her new circumstances didn't
change the way she felt about her mother's jewelry.
Each piece represented a failed hope, a guy who'd
let her mom down in the end. She wouldn't profit
from that.

A picture of her and her mom and Cooper sat
on the sideboard. Taken at their engagement party,
the shot had captured her mom in a rare moment of
unguarded laughter. Chelsea had been so aware of
her image that most photos showed her only from
her "good" side, her head tilted to erase any hint of
a double chin. It was suddenly imperative that Jorie
get the picture out of her living room. Cooper had
put that smile on her mom's face. She couldn't be
expected to keep a photo that reminded her of her
enormous failure.

She took the picture with her into the bedroom
and slid a basket off the top shelf of her closet. The
stack of cotton sweaters that had been in the basket
joined the dress and shoes on the floor. She put the
picture in instead, along with the World War II spy
novel Cooper had insisted she read. The pages were
littered with his underlinings and exclamations and
notes to himself and her. Despite the fact that she

was devouring the story, she couldn't read the rest of it with his presence on every page.

She set the basket on the bed and pulled the drawer of her nightstand open. Into the basket went the pair of glasses he'd left at her place to wear when he took out his contacts, followed by contact solution and an extra carrying case. The box of condoms went next, but then she removed it. She wasn't engaged anymore, and they were her condoms. Who knew when she might need one or twelve?

She collected two of his T-shirts and a sweatshirt from her dresser and tossed them into the basket, then headed back to the living room. She was proud that she didn't sniff any of the clothing, even though Cooper's scent—a combination of guy deodorant, paper and ink—was one of the things she'd always liked about him. Obviously, or she wouldn't have stolen the T-shirts in the first place.

The basket was now full of the odds and ends of her year-long relationship with Cooper Murphy. She flopped on the couch, the basket on the table in front of her. Their wedding binder was on top of the clothes. Cooper wouldn't want it, but then neither did she. Let him deal with it. In fact…she jerked the antique diamond ring he'd given her off her hand and tossed it on top of his stuff. Screw him. She wasn't going to start a collection of jewelry for the next generation of jilted Burke women. She didn't want any reminders of Cooper Murphy or this whole crazy year.

Except.

She slid the basket closer with her foot so she could just reach the binder without actually moving from the couch. She opened the cover and flipped past the first few pages to the archival pocket where she'd tucked Cooper's fairy tale. As soon as she had it in her hand, she remembered how she'd felt that night when he proposed. It had been wrong for them to get engaged, but she'd wanted it to be right. He'd convinced her.

Tricked her.

Loved her.

He had loved her. Or at least, she'd thought he did. She'd wanted him to. If he didn't love her, what kind of fool was she for imagining he did?

Could he have written the fairy tale for someone he didn't love? She smoothed a hand over the words on the last page, "And so on…" He'd taken it for granted that they'd live happily ever after. She hadn't, but she'd hoped.

The front doorbell chimed and she jumped, banging her knee on the coffee table and spilling a few Cheetos. Who could be at her door?

Her first thought was Cooper but she told herself not to be an idiot. He wasn't coming back. Men never did.

She put the binder in the basket. A few stray Cheetos lay on the table and she scooped them into the bowl, which she pushed under the couch with her foot before limping to the door and peering out the sidelight window.

Alice, still wearing her work clothes, a lavender bakery box in one hand, stood on her top step. She lifted the box and smiled. "Jorie?" Her voice was muffled by the heavy wooden door. "I, uh, I brought you a cake."

Alice? Alice was her friend, but not a dropping-in kind of friend. As a matter of fact, Jorie didn't have any friends of the dropping-in kind, probably because she was a private person. After a childhood spent moving and trying to fit into other people's homes and lives, she treasured the sanctuary of her own place where the only memories were ones she'd chosen. Still, Alice was her friend and she wouldn't turn her away.

"One second," she called.

Her sneakers were on the floor of the small foyer closet. She shoved her feet into them, hoping Alice would think she'd been on her way out to the gym. She slid the chain across before unlocking the dead bolt.

"Sorry for not calling first," Alice said. "But when you left I had this feeling you were going to be alone tonight, so I took the chance." She noticed

Jorie's sweats. "Oh, were you going to the gym? I can leave the cake."

Something about the way Alice was holding herself back, creating a clear dividing line between herself and Jorie's home, told Jorie that the other woman felt uncomfortable being there. Maybe dropping in wasn't something she did either. But Alice had taken a risk in coming and Jorie couldn't shoot her down.

"No. Please, come in." She stepped back and Alice handed her the cake.

"Thank goodness," Alice said while Jorie locked the door. "Eliot's incompetence was driving me insane. If I went home by myself I'd probably spend the night putting a job posting online and collecting résumés when the last thing I need is to train a new employee. If I spend some time with you, maybe the horror of Eliot will have subsided by the time I leave."

"He was kind of cute," Jorie said. "Befuddled can be endearing."

"In a koala bear, maybe. Not my counter help. He has a very beautiful boyfriend, though, who picks him up after work. If I fire him, I won't get to admire Jared anymore. I suppose my daily ogle is worth something. Your place is gorgeous." Alice glanced around the tiny foyer that opened into the living room. "I love older places like this. My condo is so new and bland...I can't help feeling it will always be superficial."

Jorie led her inside, turning on another lamp in the living room. Alice, ever-attuned to details, admired the slip-covered sofa and ran her hand across the throw pillows heaped in the corner. "Look at the trim on these pillows—I love the beading on this one. You had them made, didn't you?"

The beaded pillow happened to be one of Jorie's favorites. "I spend a lot of time in fabric stores with the brides. I've learned to indulge my passion in small amounts so I don't kill my credit cards."

Alice wandered around the living room, admiring the decor. "My place is a disaster. I keep planning to move, but it's such a pain when I'm only renting and hardly ever home anyway. You really lucked out finding this place."

Luck hadn't had much to do with it. One of her first commissions had been for an extremely uptight, image-conscious real estate developer whose daughter was three months' pregnant when she got engaged. The wedding was an enormous rush, but Jorie pulled it together and the bride was able to walk down the aisle in a nonmaternity wedding gown that managed to conceal both her baby bump and the tattoo her father hated. The poor girl couldn't take a comfortable breath, but her dad was satisfied. He gave Jorie a break on the price of the row house at the edge of the Eastern Market neighborhood. The discount, together with the entire contents of the small investment account she'd maintained, meant she could manage the down payment.

While Alice looked around, Jorie excused herself and went down the short hall that led to the bedroom. Acutely conscious of her horrid outfit, she wished she could change, but settled for pulling the door closed to conceal the messy room. Alice peeked through the open French doors to the small alcove at the back end of the house that was Jorie's office. A large, linen-covered board hung on one wall. Jorie used the space to lay out design ideas, while clear plastic boxes of samples, all carefully labeled, lined the built-in bookcases flanking the window. The *Rebel Without a Cause* concepts still covered the design wall. "What did the Richfords say about James Dean? Did they love it?"

Jorie turned toward the kitchen, holding the cake box by the string. "No. I'm quite sure that is one wedding I won't be planning. I'm definitely not getting any referral business from them either."

Alice trailed after her, apparently understanding that the Richford wedding was a closed subject. "You can have that cake for breakfast if you want. It's plain white cake, no icing. Sort of an antiwedding cake. Lots of eggs and butter to help you keep your strength up."

"You can't expect me to wait until morning for cake. Please, Alice."

Jorie had taken the doors off some of the kitchen cabinets when she repainted the kitchen, creating open display spaces where she stored the pieces she'd collected over the years.

She stretched up to a high shelf over the dishwasher, hoping Alice wouldn't notice the hole under the arm of her T-shirt, and pulled down the china cake stand she'd inherited from her mother's aunt Mae. It was white, with embossed balls like pompoms dotting the scalloped edge. When she opened the bakery box, the rich scent of the cake made her mouth water even though it looked as plain as Alice had described. She put it on the stand and got out two plates and forks.

"Do you want me to make tea?"

Alice shook her head. "I didn't mean for you to go to any trouble. Water's fine."

They carried everything back into the living room and sat down on the couch. Alice's heel hit the snack bowl and she reached down to pull it the rest of the way out. She held it up by the edge, delicately, as if it were a bowl of fish guts, before setting it on the table.

"Ah hah!" she said.

"Ah hah?"

"Ah hah, I understand what's going on. The outfit

should have been enough, but I thought you might be on your way to the gym. But sweats plus junk food equals wallowing. Perfectly understandable, I might add."

"I wasn't wallowing." She had to make the protest—she did have her pride—but was oddly glad to be found out.

"No?" Alice's eyebrows went up.

"I was depressed."

Alice frowned as she pointed with her fork at the basket full of Cooper memorabilia. "Expunging him from the record."

"I guess." Looking at the basket made her depressed for real. She'd learned as a child not to make herself too much at home in any of her temporary "uncles'" places. Cooper wasn't like that, though. He'd left little pieces of himself in every room, confident in tomorrow. Gathering those pieces up had been lonely work.

She'd been looking forward to finishing that spy novel and talking about it with Cooper. She'd already laid out the programs for the wedding with the picture of her mom, her and Cooper on the back page. Every time she saw a guy in tortoiseshell glasses, she'd think of Cooper, sitting in bed next to her, his leather notebook propped on his knees, fountain pen scratching across the page. How was she supposed to pack up all of that, her whole life with Cooper, and get rid of it? One of his T-shirts was bunched up and hanging over the edge of the basket. She pushed it back inside. She missed him already.

Jorie took a bite of cake. The texture was rich but not dense. Alice must have beaten the eggs to within an inch of their lives. The creamy butter taste was cut with just a hint of sugar. It was one of the most perfect cakes she'd ever tasted and she could barely swallow it. She put her plate on the table.

"I want him back."

The words surprised her. Not that she was thinking them. The thought had been building almost since he'd first said he was breaking up with her. But the way she said them. As if it was a done deal. As if anyone ever came back after a breakup.

Alice chewed slowly as she stared at Jorie. The declaration lingered in the air, so heavy Jorie could almost see it.

She'd dated guys before and always the breakup had included an undercurrent of relief that she could reclaim her single life. This time was different. She didn't want her old life back. She wanted Cooper. She wanted the life he'd described in her fairy tale. She wanted to love him and to have every happy moment her mom had wished for her. She wanted this awful year not to have an awful ending, but the hopeful one her mother had envisioned for her when she died.

"What's the plan?"

"I'm not sure. I need precedents. Women have been jilted before, right? What are the options for getting the guy to come back?"

And with that simple question, they were off, considering ideas and alternatives with the same connection they enjoyed when they discussed wedding plans. This was one of the reasons she'd become friends with Alice in the first place—they'd had such a good time working together professionally.

"You could pull a fake pregnancy, like in *Officer and a Gentleman*," Alice said.

"Except the fake pregnant lady is not the one Richard Gere swoops in and carries out of the factory at the end."

"I love that scene," Alice said. "It's incredibly cheesy, but I love everything about it."

"The Navy uniform helps."

"It certainly doesn't hurt. Cooper doesn't have a uniform, does he?"

"Not unless you count the lucky khakis he wears to poker night."

"What if you tried a *Pretty Woman?*" Alice tapped her fingers on her thigh. "She ends up with the guy at the end."

"What? Reinvent myself?"

"No. That won't work. She goes from street-walker to classy lady. You're already way classy. If you reinvent yourself, you'd have to become a streetwalker and we don't want that."

"Did anyone ever go from classy to trashy and still get the guy? Is that even possible?"

"*Grease* maybe. Right? Sandy swaps the poodle skirts for that slinky, full-body leotard thing and the hooker heels."

"And the gang gets together and dances their way through the senior carnival?" She'd never had the kind of optimism a movie musical required. "Cooper's no John Travolta."

"No?" Alice looked interested. "He's so tall. I assumed he'd be good at sports. Although dancing isn't exactly a sport, is it?"

"He plays baseball, but that's not really a graceful kind of game. With dancing, I always think it's almost like he never got used to being that tall." Jorie smiled, thinking about the one time they'd gone dancing together. Cooper had been so earnest, but so awkward. She pressed her hand to her top lip. She hadn't cried in such a long time, tears would almost be a relief, but they didn't come.

Alice's fingers tapped again. "Okay. No dancing."

They were both quiet for a moment. There had to be something. Some way she could get Cooper to sit up and pay attention. Some way she could convince him that no matter what he thought about her, about them, they deserved a second chance. He believed she'd been with him for the wrong reasons. She needed to get his attention so she could demand another try.

"*Say Anything.*"

"I'm thinking," Alice said.

"No. The movie. *Say Anything.* It's from 1990 or something and John Cusack is that adorable loser with the trench coat. He falls in love with the most gorgeous girl in school and he has to woo her."

"Lloyd Dobler," Alice said. "The antihero."

"Remember the boom box scene? He stands outside her window and plays that sappy song?"

"Oh, yeah. I bet wedding planners got sick of that song that year. What are you going to do, stand outside Cooper's place and hold up your iPod?"

"No. I don't mean the music. I mean Lloyd. John Cusack. It was just him, holding up the boom box and being there. He let her know he wanted her. No tricks. Right? He just went for it. Take me as I am."

Alice still seemed confused.

"I'm just going to say it," Jorie explained. "'Cooper, I want to try again.'"

"Flat out tell him?"

"Flat out."

"That doesn't leave you a back door," Alice said.

"No escape hatch or second option. If he says no, you're cooked."

"The trouble is, all the other options feel like lying or cheating or manipulating him. If I go over-the-top romantic and he says yes, I'll always wonder if he said yes to me or to the romance, because we all know he can't refuse romance. If I beg or cry, not only would I have to live with the knowledge that I'd acted just like my mom, but I'd always wonder if he said yes out of pity." Alice nodded and Jorie went on. "We got engaged the first time because of my mom's wish. This time, he has to say yes because *he* wants to. No strings attached."

There was one thing she wasn't saying. One thing she was sure no one knew because she'd done every-thing she could to keep it a secret. It was something she didn't like about herself, but had never been able to shake, no matter how many conversations she'd had with herself about growing up and living for herself and being independent. Deep down, she wanted Cooper to say yes because he wanted her. Jorie wanted to be chosen—flat out, straight up be-cause he wanted her. She'd thought that was what she'd gotten the first time. This time she was going to be utterly sure of it or she was not marrying him. Anything less would break her heart.

Not that she was planning to mention her heart.

He didn't need to know how hurt she already was. He just needed to say yes.

"You're going to have to do it in person."

"And quick. Before he tells a lot of people." She thought about Cooper telling his mom and dad or Bailey. What would they say? Would anyone try to talk him out of the decision or would they all be thankful he'd gotten out while he could? "I'll go over tomorrow morning before he leaves for work."

"Okay, you have your plan. Now let's talk about you." Alice leaned back on the couch, her hands folded across her stomach. "This afternoon you said you stink at relationships. But that's not true. You have really good friends."

"Yes, and what do they all have in common?"

"They want you to be happy?"

"None of them are my fiancé!"

Alice looked puzzled. "What does that mean?"

"You know. Men. Every serious relationship I've ever had has fallen apart because I don't know how to be in a serious relationship. I have my mom's bad example and all her baggage to tell me what not to do, but I still don't know how to do it right."

"Be yourself."

"Now you sound like a pamphlet in the middle school guidance office."

Alice pursed her lips. "You need to give yourself a break and stop thinking."

She'd already done that. The night Cooper asked her to marry him. She'd known all the reasons it was a bad idea and she'd tried to make him see that, but he wouldn't. He'd given her the fairy tale he wrote, describing the life he'd imagined for them. He'd asked her to take a leap and she had.

"I stopped thinking the first time I got engaged. I can't afford to do that again."

"Okay." Alice stood. "I disagree, but I know you'll figure this out. I'll leave the cake. It's a very nutritious breakfast."

Jorie smiled. Her mom would have had a conniption if she knew Jorie started her day with carbs. On the rare occasion that Chelsea ate breakfast, it was an egg-white omelet. That is, a single white, from a single egg, omelet. If she was particularly hungry, she might cut some chives into it.

"Cake for breakfast sounds perfect." Jorie stood, too. In fact, she was feeling quite a bit better. At the front door, Alice paused and then hugged her. Jorie wasn't expecting it, but it felt good. She squeezed the other woman back. "Thanks for coming by. I appreciate it."

"You're going to be fine, Jorie. If Cooper doesn't open his eyes and see the amazing person he's giving up, then you deserve someone better anyway. But he's going to say yes and then you'll work this out." Alice waved as she started down the steps.

Jorie was about to close the door when she heard her friend say, "Cooper! What a surprise!"

Since Jorie couldn't hear his reply, he must be a distance away.

Once she got over her shock, she realized her friend was practically shouting. Alice wanted her to know Cooper was coming down the street. *Why, why hadn't she changed her clothes?* She could have excused herself for a minute and then she wouldn't be stuck standing at the front door in these horrible sweat pants, practically screaming to the world that she'd spent the afternoon being depressed.

Maybe he wasn't coming to see her. Maybe he had errands to run at the Market or he wanted to get takeout from the Thai place on the corner or maybe he'd already met a new girlfriend and she lived on the block and they were going to run into each other all the time, nodding politely when they met on the street.

Or maybe she was going crazy. She whirled around, prepared to slam the door, but it was too late. He was there, right there on the sidewalk, walking toward her. For a guy who couldn't dance, he had a very sexy walk, understated but with an incredible shoulder and hip swagger. She swallowed.

"Jorie," he said as he came up the stone stairs.

"Cooper."

The beauty of a simple plan was it didn't need an elaborate setup or special setting. She'd planned on tomorrow, but he was here now and there was nothing to stop her from starting the rest of her life immediately.

Nothing except she wasn't dressed right. He should have called and asked her to meet him somewhere and she could have dressed in something devastating and she'd have rehearsed what to say and then she'd be in charge, instead of feeling like a complete loser in her own foyer.

This was why her mother had taught her to always consider her clothing. Chelsea had never even owned sweats and a T-shirt.

He wasn't wearing a tie and the top button of his shirt was undone. She'd told Alice the truth—he was one of the worst dancers she'd ever dated, too tall, too awkward, too aware of his own feet and not other people's, but standing in her doorway in a suit, he looked exactly perfect. He wore clothes the way a model did, as if they'd been made for him. He looked smart and strong and in charge. And that was why she'd considered maybe falling in love with him—right before he'd asked her to marry him and ruined everything.

She forgot about her sweatpants and focused on his eyes. She and Alice had organized the attack and it was the right thing to do. Bite the bullet, she thought. Do it now before he has a chance to say something that would ruin it all and send her searching for a new option. She really didn't want to have to go the Sandy-in-*Grease*-full-body-leotard route.

"I think we should get back together."

Either there was an echo in her foyer or they'd just spoken the exact same words. *In unison.*

CHAPTER FOUR

SHE LOOKED...A MESS. He didn't know what he'd expected—that he would break off their engagement and she'd go right along with her normal life? God knows that hadn't happened for him, so why should it have happened for her? This was Jorie, though. She never looked a mess. If someone had shown him that particular Dirty Bird Bar T-shirt with the holes in the shoulder seams and asked him if it belonged to Jorie, he'd have laughed. And yet, there she was wearing it along with a pair of sweatpants that had even more holes. He got a sweet glimpse of her pale thigh.

"You look great." The words slipped out, and her mouth dropped open, but he meant it. What else didn't he know about her?

He was turned-on thinking about a younger Jorie doing shots at a shore bar in that clingy T-shirt. *My God, what else don't I know about myself?*

"Can I come in?"

"No," she said, but then quickly relented. "Yes." She stepped aside and followed him into the house, closing the door behind him. In the living room, a cake stand and two crumb-covered plates were on the coffee table next to a bowl full of what looked like bright orange popcorn. The cake made sense since Alice had been there. But the orange popcorn? Jorie didn't eat junk food. There were purplish smudges under her eyes that made the blue deeper, but he couldn't remember when he'd last seen her without those shadows. Back before her mom died, he guessed.

He remembered her fingers on his wrist that afternoon. She'd held on to him. At least for that moment, she'd wanted him to stay. Was it fair to ask her to become fake engaged if she was unhappy about the breakup?

He didn't have a choice, knowing what he did about Bailey and his family, but he didn't like the way he felt right now. He'd made a mess of the situation at the bakery. He was going to have to be much more on top of his game if he wanted to convince her to go along with his plan.

She grabbed the bowl off the table and the two dirty plates and took them into the kitchen. He stayed in the living room, unsure what he was supposed to do.

"Cooper?" she called.

She walked toward him and stopped, one hand on the door frame.

"What?"

"Are you insane?"

"No." *Not yet.* But the night wasn't over and he wasn't ruling anything out at this point. Especially not when he still had to secure a fake engagement and then strategize with his dad about what really amounted to a fake appointment to the Senate.

"Well, do you have some kind of compulsive mind-changing disorder, because the only other option is that you're purposely trying to make me nuts and I know you wouldn't do that." Her voice rose as she neared him. She stopped a few steps away. The T-shirt not only had holes, it was a little too small and he could clearly see her breasts moving up and down as she breathed quickly.

She had a hot body. People didn't notice that about her right away, partly because her sophisti- cated, classy wardrobe put up such a serious front, but he suspected she hid her sexuality on purpose. Her mom had been much more feminine and overtly sexual. He'd noticed Jorie, though. It hadn't taken him more than five seconds to become aware of her curves on their first blind date. He'd expected to have to work on her for a while before he'd get his hands on her—she gave off a vibe of being con- trolled—but she'd surprised him that night. It was the one and only time he'd had sex on the first date and it had been one of the most amazing nights of his life.

"Cooper!" she said sharply, bringing his focus back to the question at hand. "Are. You. Insane?"

Her interpretation was fair. He was flip-flopping more than a congressman whose district lines had been redrawn. He wouldn't be here if not for the election, and he knew it, but he was stung by her anger, nonetheless. "I don't think so. Your opinion might differ."

She tugged on her T-shirt and glared at him. "Would you like a drink? I'm suddenly in the mood for alcohol."

The one beer he'd had in the kitchen with Bailey hadn't been nearly enough for a day like this, so he asked her for a Scotch. An antique, glass-fronted buffet on the far wall of the living room was her bar. She opened one door and pulled out two crystal rocks glasses and a small, silver ice bucket. As she crossed in front of him to get to the kitchen, she muttered, "You can sit down, you know. There's cake."

He moved to the couch, but didn't touch the cake. Instead, he watched in silence as she returned with the full ice bucket and then poured the drinks. Jorie loved formal rituals. She'd never put the ice directly into her glass if she could use the ice bucket. She'd always reach for the cake stand first and then offer you a real china plate and the right size fork. The way she moved so confidently, using the tongs to put exactly three ice cubes in her glass and leaving his straight, was typical of her. She could be wearing nothing but a garbage bag and she'd still make their drinks with a perfect country-club flourish. Her mom had taught her that presentation mattered, and he was pretty sure that for Jorie, knowing the etiquette of a situation was soothing, not stifling, the way it would be for some people. He'd always liked watching her move gracefully and competently through everyday tasks, but tonight he felt sick watching her hands. She'd already taken off his ring.

She handed his drink to him and retreated across the room to sit in the pink slipper chair near the door to her bedroom. That put the coffee table and the entire width of the Oriental rug between them. He was surprised she didn't keep going, into the bedroom or even out the window, since it seemed she couldn't stand to be near him.

He should have brought flowers. Or something. Now that he was here, facing Jorie, who was unmistakably, justifiably angry, who wasn't wearing his ring, he wasn't sure how to start. He wished he'd fleshed out the plan in his notebook, because he could use an actual opening statement right about now. She solved the problem for him by asking, "Did you really say we should get back together?"

There was no way to ease into this and no sense trying to woo her. She'd proved impervious to his romantic schemes time and again.

"Bailey has to resign. His marriage is over. He's got a girlfriend and she's pregnant. The story's going to break tomorrow at the latest." That covered the first point he'd written down. *Bailey*. Next up, his appointment to the Senate and then their need to become reengaged. Or would it be more like annulling the breakup? Either way, he'd left the hardest part for last.

JORIE TOOK A SWALLOW of Scotch. She'd only poured the drinks to have something to do while she collected herself after the shock of hearing him say they should get back together. But the news about Bailey threw her. Now that she took a better look, she saw that Cooper's knuckles were white where he gripped his glass and his shoulders slumped as if he'd been carrying something heavy and just set it down. He was really upset, and no wonder. From the first time she'd gone out for drinks with him and his brother, she'd had a crush on their relationship.

His family was defined by their legacy and place in the world. Being a Murphy from Pennsylvania meant something and everyone they met knew it.

She'd never even been remotely tempted to give up her name and take her husband's until she was engaged to Cooper. Becoming a Murphy meant she was joining a family with a history of belonging somewhere and she'd always envied families with a settled place in the world. If Bailey resigned from the Senate, where did that leave Cooper?

"I'm flabbergasted," she said. "When did you find out?"

"My dad called me in for a summit meeting right after I, um, left you at Alice's."

He moved the beaded throw pillow from behind his back and tucked it down by the arm of the couch. At least he had the good manners to look uncomfortable when he mentioned the cake tasting. This was why she hated scenes in her home. She loved that pillow, but now every time she saw it, she'd think of Cooper and his expression while he explained about Bailey. She should have made him wait while she changed so they could go out and have this crazy conversation somewhere far from her home.

"How's your mom taking it?" she asked.

"Not good."

"Your dad?"

He lifted his glass in a toast and took a long swallow.

"Bailey?"

"He's an idiot. But he's happy."

"Even though he..."

"He says he's in love."

They both took sips of their drinks to avoid having to address the question of who might or might not be in love at the moment.

"And this has something to do with our wedding obviously, since you want to rewind the whole breaking-up thing, but I'm not sure I see why." A voice inside her head was screaming for her to just take his offer. It was what she'd wanted. But she needed to know what he was thinking and exactly what she was getting into.

"My dad is on the phone right now trying to make sure I'm the appointee."

She put her drink down on the table next to her. The last thing she needed was alcohol. Her mind was spinning with everything he'd said since she opened the door, but she had a sick feeling she was starting to understand.

She got up to get a coaster from the sideboard. It gave her a chance to turn her back and compose herself before she asked her next question. She lifted her drink and put the thick glass square tile underneath it and then sat down. "Appointee to the Senate?"

He blushed. Cooper was too poised and too socially adept to blush often. In fact, the only times she ever saw him uncomfortable were when he received a compliment he wasn't able to deflect. Whatever else was going on here, he was happy about being chosen for the seat. Her mom would have eaten this news up with a spoon. Her daughter and a senator. Except…yeah. Not anymore.

"That's amazing, Cooper. You must be so proud."

He shifted again. "It's a temporary appointment. My dad wants me to hold the seat for a few months because Theo is too young to take it. He'll get the nomination for the general election, though, so I'll be out by January when he gets sworn in."

"Theo? But you have more experience than him, don't you?" While she liked Theo and there was no denying his intelligence or his wit, Cooper had been working in his brother's office for years and was already thirty-four, plenty old enough for the Senate. For a moment she forgot everything else in her irritation with Nolan Murphy. He had to be behind this. The entire family deferred to him, and he didn't, in her opinion, value Cooper enough. Bailey had always been the golden child and Cooper content to be his backup. So content that he probably hadn't even protested when Nolan declared Theo would get the job, not him.

"It's a lot of insider politicking," Cooper said. "But I have to do it, Jorie. My brother screwed up big-time. He left the entire family hanging, and if we can't hold the seat until Theo can run, I don't…I

can't see how Bay's going to be able to fix his relationship with my parents. He's going to have a baby.
Can you believe that? And I don't want him to have
to raise the kid without the family. Bailey is sick of
being a Murphy right now, but he's going to need
us. I have to do what I can to help hold the seat or
I'm afraid my parents will cut him off for good."

There was a lot about her own childhood that
had been unsettled, but the one thing she'd never
doubted was her mom's love. When Jorie was nine,
her mom had been involved with a guy who owned
a tobacco farm in Virginia, a partnership in a hedge
fund, and a racing stable in Kentucky. He traveled
every week, constantly moving to keep his thumb
on the pulse of each business. He got frustrated
when Chelsea wouldn't travel with him as much as
he wanted because Jorie was in school.

One night, she'd been up late, reading *Caddie
Woodlawn* under the covers with a flashlight,
when she'd heard her mom arguing with the guy…
Curtis was his name. Curtis wanted to send Jorie
to boarding school but Chelsea refused. There'd
been a long, tense argument. She couldn't hear
the whole thing, but her mom had repeatedly said,
"She's my daughter." They hadn't moved out right
away. Her mom's affairs rarely ended in blow-ups,
but within two months the relationship was over
and they were in Arizona, staying with her mom's

old college roommate at the spa she owned. They always ended up there when her mom was in what she called a regrouping phase.

As focused as her mother had been on finding Mr. Right, she'd put Jorie first every time. Jorie had never doubted her place in her mom's heart. She couldn't imagine how Cooper was feeling now, knowing that his parents might cut Bailey off.

She almost asked if it was a real possibility, because surely not even Nolan and Rachel Murphy would sever their relationship with a son over politics, but she didn't. Cooper believed it was possible and was throwing himself into the breach to fix the situation. Acting with his heart, not his head. She wouldn't have expected anything different. He was going to do everything he could to help keep his family together.

Even if it meant getting back together with her. She folded her arms across her stomach and waited to hear what he had to say.

"I know this is a lot to ask and I know I have no right to do it, but if I'm going to get the appointment, I can't be in the middle of a broken engagement. We don't have to actually get married. We'll postpone the ceremony and then bow out gracefully as soon as we can. The longest it would be is until after the election in November or maybe the inauguration." He was looking at the drink in his hands, not at her, as he went on with less animation. "If we break up now, with Bailey's problems in the news, it's going to be a big story. If we wait, maybe we can control the damage. No one will notice."

"Stop." She curled her fingers into the sides of her T-shirt, desperate to hold on to something. "How did this happen?" she asked quietly. If she was ever going to be able to cry again, surely this was the moment, but the tears didn't come. "How did we get to be people who have to 'control the damage' around our wedding? When we got engaged, we were in love, right?"

"We were trying to do the right thing."

"We were?" She wasn't sure she wanted him to answer. At that moment, she really wasn't sure of anything.

"Your mom was dying."

"I knew better." That was probably the thing that bothered her the most. Back when she said yes the first time, she'd known better than to agree to any idea involving her mom, a man and plans for a future. She'd known better than to trust any part of her life to another person's promises. "The main point is, you don't want to actually get back together. You want to lie for a few more months until we can break up for real. Again."

"Jorie—"

"You're not even putting any effort into it this

time. I'd have thought you'd bring flowers. You brought me flowers once because I got a parking ticket, but that was before. Now that we're lying, you don't have to try."

"You said there was no reason to spend money on flowers when you can get free samples from florists."

"So this is it. No flowers. No pretty speech. Just you asking me for a pretend engagement to save your brother."

He nodded.

"No."

"If we can just—"

"I'm not going to lie." She stood and realized she was shaking. She took a few steps toward him, hoping to settle herself down by seizing control of the situation. "Despite what you've decided, I wasn't lying when I committed to you the first time we got engaged and I'm not going to start now. I've been trying to have a relationship with you—"

He got to his feet and met her in the middle of the room. "You haven't been trying," he said emphatically. "After we got engaged, we just talked about the wedding. Our relationship stalled and nothing I've tried to do to get closer to you has worked. I booked a weekend away and you canceled at the last minute. You've spent two nights a week at the Wish Team planning the registry, and yet you never have time for dinner with me. I can't even remember the last time we had a conversation that wasn't about the wedding." His expression was bitter and disappointed and she could feel the tension as he leaned toward her.

"I can." She wouldn't back up, she was too angry. "I remember the conversation perfectly. We met for drinks after the speech Bailey gave about the education bill. We had a great time. The next night you asked me to marry you, coincidentally ruining what had been a really nice relationship."

"You said yes, Jorie. You keep saying I persuaded you, but you said yes."

How was she supposed to have said no to her mother's last wish? She'd wanted him to convince her and maybe she hadn't argued as hard as she should have, but her mom had been dying.

"I did." She had to focus on this moment, not what happened six months ago. She wanted him to understand, but it was so hard. "Which is why I'm not saying yes again."

"I need this—"

"I know." She wished she could touch him, reassure him that no matter what happened, she cared about him and didn't want to see him hurting. "That matters to me because of what you did for my mom. But still, I'm not saying yes to a lie. I can't." She meant that. She understood how much he needed this relationship, but she valued her integrity even more. If she agreed to this charade, how could she live with herself? On the other hand, if she ruined his life and Bailey's, too, how could she stand it? She wished she still had her drink. She needed something to do with her hands or she was going to reach for him. "I'll say yes if we agree we're trying for real. If we start from scratch." His chest rose as he took a deep breath and she waited to see what he'd say.

CHAPTER FIVE

WELL, THAT wasn't what he'd been expecting.

The look she gave him was definitely a challenge. He remembered it from their first blind date. They'd been set up by their mothers, who'd met at a spa in Arizona. Chelsea had been living there and Rachel had gone for a reunion with some college friends. He'd asked Jorie where she'd like to go and she suggested a trip to the Antietam Museum with that same challenge in her eye. She told him later she'd hoped the museum would scare him off. Her mom had a habit of setting her up on blind dates and she'd developed a strategy of boring the guys to death so they wouldn't call again. Instead, he'd told her he loved the Antietam Museum and she'd given him her first genuine smile, putting one hand on her hip and leaning toward him just enough that he noticed her breasts. He'd realized in that second that he was going on a date with a beautiful history geek who had a hot body and a killer smile and he'd started scheming right then to get closer to her.

He wished he could see that smile now.

"Start from scratch?" he asked. They were standing so close he could smell the faint trace of her perfume. He almost reached out to smooth a strand of strawberry-blond hair that had fallen forward. But he wouldn't touch her. Couldn't trust himself when he still wasn't sure what she wanted from him.

"We can keep the engagement, do what we have to if you're going to be appointed, pretend nothing has changed. But that's just for show. A public lie. The two of us are going to be honest and start over again from the beginning. We're not really engaged. We'll get to know each other the right way."

"How far back?"

"It's nice to meet you, Cooper." She closed her eyes and then opened them. "My name's Jorie."

"I'm Cooper— Wait, Jorie…there's no point in trying again if we don't do anything differently than before. I feel like I've tried everything and you still won't open up. I don't know what I'm supposed to do."

"You're supposed to try. I will, too. I'll change… I'll try harder. We don't have to wind up engaged for real, but we have to be honest and try."

He hated what he was doing to her. For just a second, he wondered if he should call this whole thing off. Tell his dad to find some other way. But he knew he'd already gone too far. Jorie was waiting

for his answer and he couldn't run out on her again.
She'd said she would try. She was serious.

"Deal."

Well, this was awkward. Should he stick his hand
out so they could shake on it? But Jorie was so close
to him. He thought he'd said goodbye to her for good
a few hours ago and now she was right in front of
him, wearing a shirt that was really turning him on.
If he stepped just half a foot nearer, like that…he'd
feel her against him. Her body warm and soft where
it touched his. This day had sucked, but now that
he was touching Jorie again, the bad part retreated.
He put his arms around her and bent his head to her
lips. He didn't know what to expect, what she would
want; he wasn't even sure exactly what he'd agreed
to. He started to kiss her gently, prepared to duck
out as soon as they'd sealed their agreement if that
was what she wanted, but she edged closer to him
and kissed him harder.

"Is this your way of saying you want to go all
the way back to our first date?" he murmured. Her
breasts were pressed to his chest and a rush of heat
made him shift his hands to her hips where he could
feel the flare of her backside. He found the hole in
the thigh of her sweats with his finger and touched
her soft skin. "Because I have exceptionally vivid
memories of our first date."

"That was an anomaly." Her breath on his ear

made him shiver. "I don't sleep with people on the first date."

"I don't either. And yet, there we were, on our first date, incontrovertibly doing what neither one of us ever does."

"All those museum displays about the Antietam cavalry charges had me in the mood."

Her lips parted and her tongue met his eagerly, and the instant she rubbed her hips on his erection, he couldn't stop himself from pulling her tight against him, slipping his thumbs inside the waistband of her sweats. He bit her bottom lip and then bent to kiss her neck, behind her ear and down toward her collarbone. Her hands came up and he felt them hook in the back of his belt in a possessive way that was all Jorie. He wasn't sure she realized she did it, but it made him feel that she was claiming him.

"I like first dates," she whispered. "Anything is possible."

"Anything?"

She answered him with a kiss.

He nudged her legs apart and slid his knee between them to press against her. She responded and he pulled her closer, wanting to feel her, hot and eager under his hands. If he could get her over to the couch, he'd shove all of those fussy throw pillows onto the floor and take his time, giving Jorie a night to remember.

Except he didn't have a night to give her. Not this night, anyway. He lifted his head and then, after one final stroke down her bottom, he stepped away.

"I would love to finish this," he said. Her lips were damp, and when she licked them, he shifted uncomfortably and kissed her again. "I can't believe I'm saying this, but my dad is waiting. I have to meet him."

"Is this what it's going to be like, Cooper? We're going to see each other even less than usual?"

She was quick to question his motives. Trust wasn't one of her strong suits.

"I don't think there's much chance of that. You're part of the Murphy family election machine now. My dad wants to see you tomorrow."

"For what?"

"Some might call it indoctrination. I think he'd say a briefing."

"I feel like I'm interviewing for a job."

This was hard for her. She looked nervous. She was giving a gift to his family, his brother. She had a big heart, even if it was hard for her to show it.

"You're going to be fine. I'll be there. If he kills anyone, it will be Bailey. You and I are probably safe."

"I'm not afraid of your dad, Cooper."

"Of course not."

"It feels odd, that's all. A meeting about politics seems so artificial. Before all this, I was just going to be his daughter-in-law."

"He appreciates what you're doing. I do, too." He kissed her on the cheek and then, because the subtle scent of her shampoo got him bothered again, he kissed her on the other cheek, and then because he loved the way she tasted, he moved to her mouth. She tightened her grip and the two of them sealed their deal a second time. It was a very satisfactory way to make an agreement, Cooper thought.

A few minutes later, when he was finally on his way out, he couldn't shake the feeling that he'd left something undone. He stopped in the doorway to the living room when he realized what it was.

"Do you still have your ring?"

She blushed. "Yes." She glanced away and he followed her gaze. The contents of the basket on the coffee table registered for the first time. Their wedding binder was on top, but he saw his Georgetown T-shirt underneath and the cover of the book he'd given her last week.

"That's all my stuff?"

"We broke up."

"Were you going to deliver that to me or throw it out?"

"Cooper. I was upset."

"Sorry."

He didn't want to be mad or doubt her, not when they'd just put the fragile pieces of their relationship back together, but how could she have divested herself of his things that quickly? He'd been through breakups before and he always thought there was a bit of spite involved in packing up each "memory" and returning it. He didn't want to think Jorie had done that with their relationship this soon.

It had taken less than one evening to pack him up and cut him out of her life. Cooper felt a distance slam back between them. He had to meet with his dad, but he couldn't leave her here like this.

He walked over to the basket. The ring was there, just under the binder. Jorie came up next to him, and when he held the ring up, she offered her hand. He cupped her wrist and slid the diamond over her finger.

"Okay?" he asked.

"Of course."

It wasn't much of a proposal. Nothing like his first one, that was for sure. But he felt better knowing the ring was back in place.

WHEN COOPER GOT OUTSIDE, his brother was there. He glanced up at Jorie's door but she'd already turned the lights off in the foyer. He'd hate for her to see Bailey, because she'd probably interpret his presence as more evidence that Cooper was only getting back together for his family. He walked quickly down the block, Bailey pacing him.

"What are you doing here?" Cooper asked.

"I came to check on you. How's Jorie?"

"Fine." He ducked into the grocery store on the corner. The cooler full of beer beckoned him, but he picked up a cold Coke and a bag of chips. Bailey added beef jerky and the clerk rang them up.

"So. How's the engagement treating you?" Bailey asked when they were back on the street.

"Never better," he said.

"You're a bad liar." Bailey swung around and faced him, making him stop walking. "Dad said you broke up with her this afternoon. What were you doing in there tonight?"

"Breaking up was a mistake. I got cold feet while I was writing the vows, but it's fine now."

Bailey shook his head. "Uh-uh, little brother. I know when you're lying to me. What really happened?"

"She didn't want to call it off. It was all me. After I talked to Dad, I told her I wanted to get back together. She's fine with it."

"Fine with it?" Bailey was practically shouting. He put his hand on Cooper's chest. "You're going to marry her? Didn't you listen to a single thing I told you this afternoon? It's bad enough if you want to let Dad use you to elect Theo, but you can't possibly get married for him!"

Cooper carefully stepped backward so that Bailey's hand fell away. He didn't like physical confrontations and his brother was upset. He started walking again. "I'm doing what I have to do," he said. "And Jorie knows exactly what's going on. She's fine with it. You don't need to worry." He and Jorie were stuck cleaning up Bailey's mess. His brother shouldn't be making judgments about how he did that.

Bailey wasn't following him. "Tell him no, Coop. Marry Jorie if you want to and go off and write speeches for someone you respect and don't look back. Mom and Dad can get along without the seat."

Maybe, Cooper thought. But Bailey couldn't get along without them. "We're fine, Bay," he said. "I'm going back to their house. You coming?"

There was no answer and he finally stopped and turned around. Bailey's eyes were shining in the light from the streetlamp. "I can't be with them now. Jill changed the locks at our place, but I have a key to yours. I'll let myself in if you don't mind having a houseguest for a while. I promised Dad I won't get a place with Deb until after you get the appointment."

"You know you're welcome. Take the guest room."

Bailey took a step toward him. "Don't let Dad push you around, Coop. It's not worth it."

Cooper nodded. His brother had no idea why he was doing this, but it was probably better if he could blame it on their dad instead of feeling responsible. "Don't worry. Jorie and I worked everything out. We're cool."

If by "cool" he meant completely at sea and possibly making the same mistake they'd made six months before. But this time it was because his family asked, not hers.

JORIE WASHED AND DRIED the dishes and threw away the rest of the snacks. The leftover cake fit nicely into a glass storage dish with an airtight lid. She ran a soapy cloth over the cake stand, rinsed it and then dried it. She needed a stool to put the cake stand away, then used the dish towel to dust the silver pitcher and glass vase stored on the same shelf.

Her mom had taught her to buy the best quality pieces she could afford, and if she couldn't afford quality to skip the purchase altogether. She'd also taught Jorie to care for her things because there was never a guarantee that they could be replaced. Despite the fact that she'd been making a better than decent living from her business, Jorie had held on to those old habits. She enjoyed the feeling that she had created a comfortable home for herself, and taking care of the things she'd collected was soothing.

When she finished in the kitchen, she took the basket from the table in the living room and turned off the lights before going into her bedroom. She unpacked the basket, putting each of Cooper's things away. She laid the picture frame, the spy novel, and the ring on her nightstand and then straightened up her room. The dress might have been salvageable, but she couldn't bear to wear it again so she put it in a small plastic bag and tied the top, then carried it to the trash can outside.

Her house was tidy again and locked up for the night. She was finished being depressed, which was a relief because she really wasn't cut out for the couch potato lifestyle. She got ready for bed then snuggled beneath the feather duvet, fluffing the pillows and propping them just right behind her back.

She held her hand out. There was a faint red line that showed on her finger. How long would it have taken for the line to fade, she wondered. It wasn't a question she'd be answering just yet.

Or ever, if she had anything to do with it. She'd agreed to pretend to still be engaged to Cooper. But that would end in January at the latest, after Theo was sworn in. She had the length of the campaign to be with Cooper, to get to really know him and allow him get to know her, so that in the end they wouldn't want to let each other go. Once they'd discharged their obligation to his family and they were free to separate, she hoped he'd be ready to say yes for real.

She slid her ring back on. Cooper had given it to her a few days after they got engaged. It was a Civil War–era antique, a pretty gold band engraved with roses and set with a round diamond. Even her mom had approved of it. The inscription inside the band read simply "Dearest" with the year 1863. She stood the picture of her and her mom and Cooper on the night table and opened the book on her lap.

Before she started reading, she closed her eyes. She missed her mom. When Chelsea had first called to tell her about the delightful woman she'd met at the spa and the delightful woman's eligible son who would be calling Jorie for a date, Jorie had felt impatient. Her mom had been diligently sending men her way and just as diligently ignoring her daughter's repeated requests to stop. When her first date with Cooper went so well, she'd called her mom to thank her. Chelsea had been appalled that she'd sent Jorie a Civil War history buff. Her exact words were, "His mother said he was in politics. She didn't say he was a nerd."

"It's going to be okay, Mom," Jorie whispered into the silent bedroom. "Keep an eye on us, okay?"

She waited, but she didn't get a response. Opening the book, she started to read.

JORIE STOPPED AT LUCKY'S on her way to her meeting with Nolan. Alice was behind the counter. There was a line of five customers, and a Help Wanted sign in the window.

Alice looked harried, but when she saw Jorie, she raised her eyebrows. Jorie lifted her hand, flashing the engagement ring with a smile. Alice gave her a quick thumbs-up before she went back to helping a mom who was juggling two toddlers.

Jorie waited while Alice packaged a dozen cupcakes, sorted out the next three people who wanted muffins and coffee to go, and then described the ingredients of practically every pastry in the case to a middle-aged woman who sounded as if she were almost asleep from boredom. When the woman finally bought an apple pie, Jorie almost shouted, *If you were in the mood for apple pie, why not just buy it?*

Alice waited until the door of the bakery closed behind the woman before she muttered a curse word. "I need to get some help in here before I go crazy."

"You didn't fire Eliot, did you?"

"Eliot's job is safe because he's currently the only thing standing between me and a total meltdown.

My full-time counter help, Nicole, quit. Her daughter's pregnant with her fifth kid and she had to go on bed rest. Nicole's watching the other kids for her. Which means it's me and Eliot. He's still not brilliant and he's in school full-time, but he's all I've got. Eliot is now the Lucky's Bakery Employee of the Month." Alice flipped over the Open sign on the front door so it read Closed for Lunch and then she turned the lock. "Come in the back and tell me everything!"

"I can't stay," Jorie said. "But the very short version is we're back together."

"I never believed he wanted to break up with you in the first place!"

Jorie didn't correct her. She'd decided to start the day off with a positive attitude. She'd wanted Cooper back and now she had him. The why couldn't matter. It was up to her to convince him that they weren't making a mistake before time ran out.

"What do you have that's a foolproof hit with guys?" she asked.

"For Cooper?"

"His dad."

Alice stood in front of the counter and examined the options. "Not cupcakes. Not croissants. Not muffins. Pie's too messy and you can't tell about fruit desserts, anyway."

Jorie waited. If everything worked out, she'd be

spending so much time with the Murphys that she'd know their dessert preferences inside and out, but today she was going to have to trust Alice.

"Chocolate chip cookies," Alice said. She went behind the counter and grabbed a box. "Men like things uncomplicated."

"They do?"

"They think they do, anyway." Alice loaded the box and then wrapped it with string. "Call me later, would you? I'd love to hear the long story."

"Okay." Jorie took out her wallet but Alice waved her hand.

"It's an engagement present."

Jorie dropped a dollar in the tip jar. "You can give that to Eliot. Butter him up so he doesn't quit on you."

"Flip the sign back when you leave, okay?"

Jorie nodded and picked up the box. Nolan Murphy was waiting and she didn't want to be late.

CHAPTER SIX

COOPER'S APARTMENT, a quiet two-bedroom on a shady street with a tiny kitchen but working windows, had gone from just right for one single guy to seriously stuffed with Murphys. When Cooper got home from Jorie's the night before, Bailey was sleeping in the extra bedroom and Theo had installed himself on the couch. His cousin swore he wouldn't be there long and not even every night. He and Nolan had decided it made sense for him to be briefed right along with Cooper, but he was only taking a partial leave from his firm. He'd work remotely, going back to Pittsburgh a few times a week when he had to be on-site. When he was in Washington, he and Cooper would be joined at the hip and Bailey, despite his disgrace, would be right along with them, offering his insights and attempting to look both contrite and not that guilty, while the governor and the public made up their minds about the Murphy Issue.

At least those were the details his brother and cousin had given him once they were out of bed and shuffling around the small table in the galley kitchen. When Theo and Bailey started arguing over who got to do the crossword puzzle in the *Times,* he left. He was supposed to meet his dad and Jorie at ten. He had about two hours and he didn't want to be early—he didn't want to listen to any of his dad's plans just yet. Even if he went somewhere for coffee, he'd still have to figure out how to fill more than an hour. Maybe he should stop by Jorie's and see if she wanted to go together.

The sidewalk outside his building was shaded by a line of cherry trees and the wooden benches set at intervals down the block were mostly empty. He registered the woman in the over-sized sunglasses and head scarf wrapped like a fifties starlet. She was sitting on the bench closest to his steps and reading a magazine, but he didn't really see her. Some part of his brain must have been paying attention though, because after he'd gone a few steps past her, he realized two things. One, the woman was dressed like some kind of femme fatale in a James Bond film from her trench coat to her glasses, but she was reading the *Wall Street Journal.*

"Mom?"

"Cooper," she said with a grim smile he was pretty sure she meant to be significantly brighter. Maybe if she didn't grit her teeth so tightly she'd have been able to pull off delighted. As it was, she looked just as furious as she had the day before. She slid the sunglasses partway down her nose. "What a surprise."

"You're surprised to see me outside my building?"

"No. I mean, yes." His mom closed the newspaper and tucked it into the front pocket of her big leather satchel. "I'm surprised to see you. I thought you might have spent the night at Jorie's."

"You could have rung the doorbell if you wanted to talk," he said.

She didn't answer him and he finally caught on.

"You're stalking Bailey, aren't you?"

"No."

"Those are stalker sunglasses," he said. "The scarf is definitely a stalker scarf. It looks good on you, though."

"Thank you. And don't contradict your mother." She lifted the glasses back up to cover her eyes again.

He took the spot next to her. Sitting side by side on the bench, he wouldn't have to see the brittle hurt and anger in her face as she tried to pretend she didn't care about her first born son's existence.

He wasn't sure what to say so they sat in silence for a few minutes. The traffic was starting to pick up and a few groups of kids walked past, heading for the middle school around the corner.

"I followed the bus when he went to kindergarten the first day, you know." Rachel undid the knot on her scarf and took it off, folding the silk over and around her hand. "You, too. You tell yourself you're ready, that your child is ready, that it's only school and millions of kids have been completely happy there before." She shrugged, a small movement of her shoulders that was apologetic and embarrassed in a way his mom rarely was. "But then the bus pulls away and it feels like you've lost some important part of you. Like you might float away because there's nothing keeping you on the ground. Bailey wasn't gone more than thirty seconds when I knew I had to follow the bus, just to see. To be sure he was okay. I parked across the street and watched him go in. I just had to see."

"Bailey's okay, Mom," Cooper said.

"You've met Deb?"

It was a question, but not really. She was prepared to be hurt all over again when she confirmed that he'd been lying to her right along with Bailey.

"No."

She turned her head and took the glasses off again. There were tears in her eyes.

"I still remember the time you attempted to cover up for your brother when he told Theo we had a dungeon in the basement and the poor child fell down the stairs carrying that jug of water for the prisoners."

"I had to lie. Bay didn't deserve to get into trouble because Theo was the world's most gullible six-year-old. But I'm not lying to you now, Mom. I haven't met her."

"He's been very thorough about keeping us out, hasn't he?"

Cooper rested his hand on his mom's forearm and squeezed. "He probably thought he was protecting us, right? If we didn't know, we wouldn't have to lie about it."

She unwound the scarf from her fist and then tucked it into her bag.

"Your dad says you and Jorie broke up and got back together yesterday. Apparently you'd already broken up with her when you told me you liked the red velvet cake."

And there it was. He wasn't lying about Deb, but was guilty of this one.

"I didn't mean to lie to you, Mom. I just didn't know how to tell you."

"And then?"

"And then we got back together."

"Coincidentally just after you found out we need you to run for the Senate."

"Dad was clear that I'm not running. I'm being appointed."

"Semantics."

Except it wasn't. Theo was the candidate and Cooper was just the fill-in. All of this, getting back together with Jorie when he didn't see much hope for their relationship, was only to buy Theo the few months he needed to hit the right age to be the candidate. Theo was the chosen one. Cooper wondered if he'd go back to being a speechwriter when this was all done. Would he be able to work for Theo? Would his cousin even want him?

"I told Jorie the truth. She knows we have to stay together for the campaign and she's okay with it."

Rachel crossed her legs as another group of kids went past. One of them was on a scooter and he swished by so close Cooper pulled his feet back against the bench.

"I hope you were honest with her, Cooper. She's been through so much this past year, losing her mom. We all know what needs to be done, but Jorie isn't a Murphy."

She almost was, Cooper thought. What would that have felt like, he wondered, to have a branch of the Murphys that was his alone. Would it have been a refuge? A home base? A retreat? Or a burden? He wouldn't know now, at least not with Jorie. There was no way a relationship could go through as much as theirs had and ever wind up healthy, but he still wondered. He'd told her he would try again, start from scratch, but there was an awful lot of complicated history between them.

"When are you meeting your dad?" Rachel asked.

"Ten."

"I have an errand to run, but I should be home before eleven."

She stood and he got up, too. Rising on her tiptoes, she kissed his cheek. "Take care of yourself, Coop."

"You, too."

She faced away from his front door as she got her glasses back out and put them on.

"Bailey's still home, if you want to stop by," he said, doing his best to keep his tone neutral so she wouldn't feel judged. His mom didn't deal well with ultimatums, especially from her sons.

"Not today," she said.

When she walked away, her back was straight and her stride as firm and energetic as ever, and he knew it wasn't possible that she actually looked a little smaller, as if she'd lost something.

He was doing the right thing. He had to get this appointment and keep the seat ready for Theo. It was the only hope he had for his family to get back to normal.

* * *

JORIE HAD DRESSED for this meeting with a specific goal in mind. Cooper's mom tended toward romantic, very feminine clothes, but with her own distinctive style.

Although Jorie hadn't tried to replicate Rachel's style exactly, she'd chosen a cute cotton skirt printed with black-and-white flowers and paired it with a shimmery charcoal summer sweater with a trio of white flowers on the shoulder. She hoped her clothes delivered the subtle message to Nolan that she was prepared to support Cooper in the same way that Rachel supported her husband.

The weight she'd gained after her mom died had made some of her clothes uncomfortably tight, but the shape of this skirt and the silky weave of the sweater actually looked better with more curves underneath. She felt good and that was important because she was nervous. When she told Cooper she wasn't intimidated by his dad, it was the truth—at least, she wasn't any more intimidated by Nolan Murphy than anyone else was. What scared her was how much this meeting meant to Cooper. With everything he was doing to keep his family together, she was petrified that she would mess something up.

She crossed the street and approached the Murphys' house. The lace curtains in the front windows were lined with opaque fabric which meant she couldn't see inside. Somehow, she didn't imagine Nolan would be watching for her from the front window. In fact, she was kind of surprised he wanted to meet her at the house. He was so busy prepping for the transition, she'd been under the impression he'd be living at Bailey's office all day.

The stone steps and banister leading to the highly polished front door were old, solid and smooth with age. She wondered if Cooper ever thought about the people who'd lived here before him. He'd grown up splitting his time between this house and the equally old and impressive one his parents kept outside Philadelphia.

Both homes had been in his family before he was born. This had been his grandparents' place when his grandfather was in the Senate. Cooper and Bailey had grown up with the kind of stability and tradition she'd longed for when she was a child, shuffling from city to city. She'd changed schools so often it had almost become a routine. Cooper told her once that at Christmastime his family didn't have to think about where to hang the stockings on their living room fireplace because the holes were there, in exactly the same spots they'd always been. She wondered if he knew how lucky he was.

At the bottom of the steps she paused and thought about her mom. Chelsea had always known what to

wear and had never brought a hostess gift that was
less than perfect. Jorie hoped her mom could see
her right now. She hoped even more that Chelsea
would approve. Her nerves weren't going to settle
themselves, so she rang the bell and hoped for the
best. At least she had Alice's cookies with her. They
should smooth the way.

When Bailey answered the door, she was so relieved it was him and not his dad that she smiled
before she remembered the turmoil in his life that
was the reason she was there.

"Bailey, I'm so sorry for everything that's going
on."

"Actually, I think I'm the one who should be
apologizing to you," he said. He held the door open
and stepped back. Once she was inside, he leaned
down and kissed her cheek. He put his hands on her
shoulders. "You know you don't have to do this."

Over his shoulder, she saw Nolan and Cooper
come to the doorway of the library down the hall.
Nolan's face was set and he didn't smile, just nodded
and folded his arms. Cooper, standing behind him,
his brown eyes serious, looked very much like his
dad at that moment. Jorie was struck by how close
the three of them had always seemed—working
together, joking together, sharing their family and
their history. Now there was a rift and Cooper had
asked her, trusted her to do what she could to mend

it. The Murphys might be messed up at the moment, but she believed in them. She pulled Bailey in close for a hug, sliding one arm around his waist while she held the cookie box in her other hand.

"Yes, I do," she whispered. "I want to."

She heard footsteps and saw Cooper coming down the hall, his long legs covering the distance so quickly she barely had time for a deep breath to steady herself.

"You brought us cake," he said, taking the box she held out to him. "You're a goddess."

"It's cookies," she said. "And Alice is the goddess, but I'm glad they're welcome."

Cooper put his arm across her shoulders to steer her down the hall toward his father, but she pulled away and went back to Bailey. She took his hand in hers and leaned up to kiss his cheek. "Congratulations on the baby," she said softly. "I'm looking forward to meeting your girlfriend."

He finally gave her a grin that wasn't quite up to his normal magazine-ready smile but seemed sincere. "We'll set that up. Definitely."

"Cooper, Jorie—let's get started," Nolan called. "Bailey, I'll need you in about thirty minutes, but you can take a break for now."

Jorie grabbed the cookie box back from Cooper. She wasn't going to miss her chance to bribe his dad herself. As she walked down the hallway, she felt Cooper behind her and was glad he was there. She had said she wasn't intimidated and she really shouldn't be, but facing this grim, serious Nolan felt different. Every other time they'd been together, it had been social, but now she was part of the family business and she didn't know quite what to expect.

NOLAN THANKED HER for the cookies, put them next to him on the table, unopened, and handed her a list.

"Dad, maybe we should talk first, sort of ease into things," Cooper said.

Nolan handed him a list.

Cooper opened his mouth as if he were about to protest again, but Jorie said, "This is just fine. We have lots to cover." She set her bag down on the table and took her pen out of the inside pocket. "Let's get started."

Cooper pulled out a chair at the library table, and after she sat down, he settled into the one next to her, but she noticed that he left one hand on the back of her chair. This was just a conversation about politics, but it was kind of him to make the protective gesture and she relaxed slightly.

"The first thing is the media. Bailey's holding a press conference at one o'clock tomorrow. He'll resign then. Karloski has remarks prepared, but he's not going to appoint Cooper right away. Says he has questions."

"Questions?" Cooper said. "What questions?"

"We're not sure. He's not talking. Yet."

"Is he going to come through, though? Is this a power thing? Making us wait to remind us he's in charge?"

Nolan bent over the table. "We don't know, Cooper. By law he can take six weeks. We hope he's not going to wait that long and I know the party's leaning on him. I just hope he gets his mind straight quick because the sooner we get you appointed, the sooner we can get Theo campaigning." He shook his head. "I never thought I was going to have to sell you as a viable alternative to your brother, that's for sure."

If she hadn't been watching Cooper carefully just then Jorie would have missed his slight flinch.

"Maybe you'd have done something about that B-I got in Algebra I, if you'd known," Cooper said.

Nolan pressed his lips together.

"If the governor's not ready to go right away," Jorie said, "it means we have a few days in between Bailey's announcement and Cooper's, right?"

Nolan nodded.

"I'm going to need to work things out with the Wish Team—sort out a postponement date and decide how to handle the registry, because some of the wishes can't be put off. Maybe I can get that going while we're waiting for the governor."

"Whenever you talk to anybody, make sure you stick to the points on the memo. Your engagement should be covered on page two."

Jorie flipped to the second sheet and saw her relationship with Cooper laid out in bullet points. The first bullet was about Cooper's duty to his family. Next came their mutual impatience to marry followed by their mutual understanding that they needed to wait. The last two bullets were about looking forward to a lasting marriage and the wedding, which would happen at some undefined point after the election. Bailey's relationship with Jill was similarly outlined from the current "difficult situation" through a trial separation, but it didn't end as well as her list. At the bottom were about five items titled "Cooper's Qualifications." The third sheet was all about Theo.

She glanced at Cooper. One finger skimming over the page, he scanned his list.

"The press is going to try to catch you alone, Jorie," Nolan continued. "They're going to want dirt on Bailey and Jill. Don't talk to anyone you don't know. Don't talk to anyone you do know about this, unless it's someone on our team. Do not speak about Deb or the baby ever. If you run into problems or

Send For
2 FREE BOOKS
Today!

I accept your offer!

Please send me two free
Harlequin® Superromance®
novels and two mystery
gifts (gifts worth about $10).
I understand that these books
are completely free—even
the shipping and handling will
be paid—and I am under no
obligation to purchase anything, ever,
as explained on the back of this card.

About how many NEW paperback fiction books have you purchased in the past 3 months?

❏ 0-2
FC9W

❏ 3-6
FC99

❏ 7 or more
FDAL

❏ I prefer the regular-print edition
135/336 HDL

❏ I prefer the larger-print edition
139/339 HDL

Please Print

FIRST NAME

LAST NAME

ADDRESS

APT.#

CITY

STATE/PROV.

ZIP/POSTAL CODE

Visit us online at
www.ReaderService.com

Offer limited to one per household and not applicable to series that subscriber is currently receiving.
Your Privacy—The Reader Service is committed to protecting your privacy. Our Privacy Policy is available
online at www.ReaderService.com or upon request from the Reader Service. We make a portion of our mailing
list available to reputable third parties that offer products we believe may interest you. If you prefer that we not
exchange your name with third parties, or if you wish to clarify or modify your communication preferences, please
visit us at www.ReaderService.com/consumerschoice or write to us at Reader Service Preference Service, P.O. Box
9062, Buffalo, NY 14269. Include your complete name and address.

HD-SR-F11 ◄ Detach card and mail today. No stamp needed. ◄ © 2010 HARLEQUIN ENTERPRISES LIMITED ® and ™ are trademarks owned and used by the trademark owner and/or its licensee. Printed in the U.S.A.

make a mistake, tell us. Don't hope it will go away, because it won't—it will only get worse."

Jorie nodded along with him even though she felt as if she'd dropped into some B-movie spy flick. Surely this wasn't necessary.

"Your job is okay," Nolan said, "but be sure you vet your clients. We don't need someone posing as a bride when they're really out to do a story on you. Make sure you're appropriately dressed at all times unless you want a picture of you in your ratty sweatpants to show up on the cover of a gossip rag. It goes without saying that you won't drink to excess, do drugs, or engage in any kind of activity that will reflect badly on Cooper."

"Dad!" Cooper said. "That's enough."

"I don't think she's going to do any of this, obviously, but if you're not used to being in the public eye, you're not used to thinking about how you look all the time. It's important if we're going to pull this off."

"Jorie's never been anything but completely trustworthy and lovely. You know her."

"I know your brother and look at the mess we're cleaning up this week."

Cooper pushed his chair back and stood, pulling Jorie up with him. She couldn't remember ever hearing him raise his voice to his father before. "Are we finished?"

Nolan straightened the papers in front of him as if he wanted to continue, but he glanced at Cooper and rolled the pages into a tube. He gave it three quick, decisive raps on the table and then said, "Jorie, do you know what we need?"

She nodded.

"Can you be that person for us?"

"Yes," she said, even though she felt queasy. "Yes, I can."

Cooper held her arm and she could tell he wanted to talk but she couldn't face him just then. She excused herself and went to the small downstairs powder room off the kitchen. The room had been sliced out of the former butler's pantry and was tiny but perfectly decorated with two wallpaper prints and a porthole-style mirror. It always reminded her of a room from a dollhouse. She relished the intimacy now as she fought to control her feelings.

The things Nolan had said reminded her strongly of talks she'd had with her mom as a child. They'd restyled themselves for each new guy her mom pursued. One year Chelsea would be the perfect Junior League member, hosting parties for charities and sending bread and butter thank-yous on engraved stationery for all the brunches and dinners she attended. Another year, she was sporty—spending her days at the country club on the golf course or the tennis court. When Jorie was in the seventh grade, they'd spent the year in London and Jorie relished the opportunity to immerse herself in historical sites, while her mom spent time at art auctions and gallery openings.

Jorie had sworn the day she went off to college that she would never let a man's whims dictate who or what she was. She didn't blame her mom—Chelsea had made her choices and Jorie made different ones, that was all.

She turned on the cold water and then leaned on the sink with both hands. Cupping water in her palm, she splashed her face a few times. The soft hand towel soothed her when she dried her skin.

She wasn't doing the same thing her mom had done. Sure, Nolan had a list and he expected her to live within its parameters, but she still had her own life. Didn't she? She would follow Nolan's rules and stick to the bullet points for now, but only because Cooper loved his family and she owed him a really big favor. She wasn't giving up her freedom for this relationship. The arrangement was temporary. It would be okay.

When she left the powder room, Bailey told her Cooper had gone upstairs so she went to find him. The walls along the stairway were lined with family photos and she searched for Cooper in each one, smiling when she picked him out of a collection of cousins around a Christmas tree. In another photo—probably taken on the first day of school—he had an adorable bowl cut and two missing front teeth. The pictures were lovely and it wasn't until she got to the top landing that she realized they were all carefully staged. There wasn't a single hair out of place or a mismatched outfit anywhere on that wall.

The Murphy family story was a serious business, judging by the photos they chose to display.

She hadn't been upstairs at the Murphys' house before, and for a moment she wasn't sure where to turn, but there were only five doors off the long straight hall and one was open.

She knocked lightly and then pushed the door open. Cooper was stretched out on a quilt covering an antique bed, his shoulders propped against the walnut headboard. His room was dark and masculine with a set of heavy bureaus and a desk that matched the bed. The wall next to the door was lined with overstuffed bookcases. She wondered if the bedroom had looked like this when Cooper was a child or if Rachel had redecorated when he'd gotten older. The wooden shutters at the windows were open now, letting light stream in, but she thought the room might seem spooky to a small child.

He patted the bed. "Want to hide out with me for a few minutes?"

She sat next to him, scooting back until her shoulder rested comfortably on his chest. When he put his arm around her shoulder, she relaxed into him. He was warm and familiar in a day that had gotten off to a disconcerting start.

COOPER HADN'T FELT THIS angry with his dad in a long time. He knew the guy was under stress and he was going to cut him some slack because of it, but that session with Jorie was not going to be repeated.

After she was settled next to him, he said, "I'm so sorry. My dad was out of line."

"I told you, it's okay."

"It's not, Jorie. I'm going to talk to him. You're not an employee, for God's sake."

He squeezed her shoulder because that statement made him uncomfortable. She wasn't an employee, but they did have a business deal, didn't they?

"He didn't single me out, you know. You have a list, too, and it's very similar to mine."

"That's different."

"Different how?"

He realized it wasn't really different just because he was used to his dad blurring the line between family and work didn't mean it wasn't obnoxious. He settled for a shrug since he couldn't answer her question.

"Cooper, we have to get past this. We're never going to be able to act naturally with each other unless we can acknowledge that there is an artificial basis for our relationship right now."

"But?"

"But after Theo gets elected, then we can find out how we really feel. We have some time, don't we?"

"Yes."

"So let's pretend yesterday at Lucky's never happened. We're still engaged and that's all that matters, right?"

"Okay."

She leaned over him to look at his notebook. "What are you working on?"

"Bailey's resignation speech."

"I thought you'd be finished with that by now."

He pulled his arm away and got up. The top shutters were still closed so he opened them.

"I can't get it down. Every time I start, I hear him telling me he's sick of being Bailey Freaking Murphy and I can't write the words. Anything I write is a lie."

Jorie swung her legs off the bed so she was sitting on the edge. "Don't take this the wrong way, but haven't you written lies before?"

"Not lies. I mean, we spin things, but I haven't knowingly lied. He cheated, Jorie. He went behind

Jill's back and slept with another woman. I know he's in love and he felt trapped, but the truth is, he shouldn't have done it."

"And you're angry with him."

Cooper had a picture of him and his family at Bailey's college graduation. He took it over to Jorie and handed it to her. "You see how my parents are looking at him?"

She nodded.

"That's how everybody looked at him, all the time. You know. He's got something special. He is something special."

"You think he's throwing that all away?"

Cooper glanced down at the picture in her hands. "I know it's not fair for me to expect him to be something he doesn't want to be, but he let it go too far. Why didn't he say no back when he was twenty or twelve or—" He knew he sounded whiny. He wasn't whining. He wished Bailey the best. "I just hate that the rest of the family is out of whack now."

Jorie set the picture on the bed next to her and stood up. "Did you ever wonder why it was Bailey and not you?"

He shook his head. "Not once."

"And now? When the job is going to Theo? Do you wonder why it's him and not you?"

He cupped her face and kissed her softly. "Have

you met my dad? There's no point in wondering something like that."

She leaned up to kiss him again. "I wonder that, Cooper. I think your dad is missing out."

"Missing out on what?"

"On you. Why are they passing you over to nominate Theo? Did they even ask if you want the job?"

"No."

"Why not?" she snapped.

Cooper realized she was angry on his behalf. She had accepted his dad's rude behavior toward her, but this was the second time she'd brought up the idea that he should be the candidate. He studied her—her hands were balled into fists and her shoulders were pulled back. She was really mad.

He captured her hands and lifted them to his lips. "Thank you, Jorie," he said. "For thinking of me as candidate material."

"But?"

"But I don't want to be a senator."

"As long as you're sure it's you making the choice and not them."

He didn't know how to respond to that. He had his job to do and that was what he needed to focus on. The last thing his family needed was to have him suddenly veer off course.

"Second-guessing isn't going to get this speech written," he said.

"So what would you say? If you were going to explain all this to me, what would you say?"

He was angry at Bailey. The part of him that was Bailey's brother understood, but the part that had been writing speeches for Pennsylvania's senator for most of his adult life was furious.

"Everything my dad wants me to say sounds like a lie. It's all politics, but I don't think people want to hear spin when they've been hurt."

"Your dad's not the speechwriter. You are. What do *you* want to say?"

"That Bailey's sorry. That he understands why people are mad. That there's a plan."

"So say it. Tell it to me like you want to tell it to the people back home."

"I think Pennsylvania deserves a senator who's totally focused on the issues and challenges currently..."

Jorie crossed her arms under her breasts as she listened to him, and he wasn't quite as angry with Bailey as he had been. It was hard to stay focused when you were tempted by a beautiful woman.

"Um...I think Pennsylvania has a long history of loyalty and roots in integrity and honor. I think Pennsylvania understands family and my family understands Pennsylvania. Bailey is ready to move on to a new chapter in his life, but that doesn't mean that the voters aren't owed exactly the type of dedication, power, and influence they chose when they elected Bailey. If they can find it in their hearts to understand Bailey's new path, they will find that the Murphy family is ready to walk into the future with them once again."

When he was finished, she kissed him again. "You want to write that down while it's fresh?"

"I swear, Jorie, I couldn't get a word on paper after I talked to my dad yesterday."

"It's okay to be angry with him, Cooper. It's okay to be angry with any of them. You're doing the right thing for yourself and that's what matters." She put the picture back on his bookcase. "I'm going to head out now. You finish your speech and we'll see what comes next, right?"

After she was gone, he sat at his desk. Well, it wasn't his desk anymore, but he'd spent an awful lot of time working there when he was a kid. He wrote the speech in longhand because he always thought better with a pen than a keyboard. The whole time he heard Jorie's voice in his head, wondering why it was Theo's turn now and not his. If they'd offered him the job, would he have taken it? He hadn't even considered that possibility before today.

He didn't want to be a senator. He knew where his talents lay. They were with pen and ink, papers and imagination. The day-to-day grind of legislation and committees would kill him. Still, he wondered why they hadn't asked. They simply assumed that he would do what he was told for the good of the family, and they were right. But what did that say about him?

When Theo was elected and he stepped aside, what would be waiting for him?

CHAPTER SEVEN

THE NEXT DAY, Jorie waited outside the Wish Team offices for Cooper to arrive. She would have gone in by herself, if the appointment had been anywhere but here, where everything was so tied to memories of her mom. She didn't want to face it alone.

Cooper came around the corner, his walk strong and sexy, and she immediately felt better. There was only one person left in the world who knew how much the Wish Registry meant to her mom, and now that he was here, she could have this meeting.

MIRIAM JENNINGS WAS THE senior gifts coordinator at the Wish Team. Once Jorie and Cooper decided to donate their gifts and Chelsea had dreamed up the registry, she'd been brought in to consult with them and mesh their wedding gift registry with the tenth anniversary celebration.

After Chelsea could no longer help, Miriam and Jorie had spent endless hours attempting to match donations to wishes. Miriam's cramped office with the untidy metal desk was as unpretentious as she was, and although Chelsea had at first been put off by the lack of glamour, she and Jorie both had come to have enormous respect for the earnest, creative, and resourceful Miriam. To say the coordinator was disappointed that they were postponing their wedding was an understatement.

Miriam was devastated. Her lovely apple-pink cheeks and bouncy black curls actually seemed to deflate. "We've received over a hundred and fifty gifts already," she said. "We'll have to give them all back."

Jorie was sympathetic. She'd felt that same panic and loss when she first started thinking about the registry after Cooper broke up with her, but they'd come up with a solution. Miriam had nothing to worry about.

"We don't think so. Cooper's written up a notice we can send out to everyone, letting them know that even though the wedding is on hold, we're hoping they'll still fulfill the wishes now, when they're needed."

Miriam didn't look any less worried.

"There might be a few people who pull out," Jorie rushed to reassure her, "but Cooper's parents have agreed to fund any lost wishes. We are committed to making this happen."

Cooper had a copy of the note printed up and he passed it across the desk to Miriam. He looked uncomfortable, too tall for the small folding chair he sat in. Jorie was positive the note would be a winner. He'd struck just the right balance between letting folks know they weren't under any obligation to fufil their pledge and clearly stating the some poor person who was looking forward to receiving their wish would be horribly let down if they didn't.

Miriam shook her head. "You don't understand, Jorie. You haven't said it in so many words, but I live in Washington. It's obvious Cooper's running for his brother's Senate seat. We can't take these donations now, not if he's a candidate for office." She pulled a tissue out of the box on the corner of her desk. "I was so afraid this was why you called the meeting. Crap."

Hearing Miriam use such a word was a shock. That she'd quickly guessed what was behind their postponement was another shock. She looked so convinced the whole registry was a no-go that Jorie felt sick to her stomach. She hoped her mom wasn't looking down on this meeting.

"Nobody said I'm running for anything," Cooper objected.

Miriam shrugged. "So tell me you're not."

"I respect you too much to lie to you, Miriam," he said. "But please, it's vital that the assumptions you've made today don't leave this office."

"We're under the confidentiality clause. Any

conversation I have with donors over the circumstances and timing of their gifts is private and remains that way."

"And speculation about my brother?"

"Is rampant. It's Washington, Cooper, and he's Bailey Murphy. But everything we're talking about here is confidential and will stay that way." Miriam dabbed at her eyes. "I can't believe the timing. I just can't."

"I don't understand." Jorie had gotten lost somewhere around the time Miriam started crying.

"There are rules about donations," Cooper said, his voice subdued. "I should have remembered. If people give me gifts now that I'm going to be appointed, they all have to be reported and counted. If they were regular wedding gifts, it wouldn't be a big deal, but some of the wishes cost too much. They won't be allowed at all because of who donated them. Crap."

And now Cooper was using vulgar expressions in front of Miriam? It was as if the world was ending right here in front of her eyes.

"No," Jorie said. "We're having the Wish Registry." She felt like stomping her foot. "This registry is my mom's legacy. Our wedding was her wish and you filling it was a huge joy to her, Miriam, you know that. But the registry is going to touch people. It's going to let my mom's spirit live on, the part of her that wanted everyone she knew to be happy. My mom's idea will help people. I'm not letting it end before it even really gets started. My mom deserves this to go ahead."

Miriam handed her a tissue even though she was too angry to cry.

"Jorie, there are laws," Cooper said. "It's not possible—"

"No," she said again. "Miriam, if you'll excuse us, I need to speak to Cooper outside."

"Everything you say is confidential," Miriam reminded her, but Jorie shook her head. This wasn't about confidentiality, it was about her jumping out of her skin if she couldn't get up and move around while she figured this mess out.

Cooper had the door open for her and he followed her down the hall, easily keeping pace with her angry strides. Outside the building, she took a left and detoured around a group of teenage girls with shopping bags and cell phones before she ducked into the parking lot.

"I'm sorry if I sound like a two-year-old," she began, "but I'm not listening to 'not possible' or 'can't' or anything else that means this Wish Registry isn't going to happen. Enough of my life is caught up in the Murphy family political sideshow. My mom's registry is not going to fall prey to it." His silence during the walk from Miriam's office hadn't been encouraging and his expression now looked more unhappy than anything else. She felt her initial anger slipping into despair. She couldn't lose everything her mother had wanted, could she? So she said something she knew was a low blow. "She trusted you."

He blinked. For Cooper, this was probably worse than being hit. He knew very well what it meant when she said her mom had trusted him. Chelsea had spent her life making one bad bet after another when it came to men. Her very last bet had been in Jorie's name, on Cooper. How could he, the born romantic, stand to let Chelsea down again?

"I don't want to hear one more word about laws. We're not dummies, Cooper. You put your heart to work and I'll put my mind to work and we'll solve this."

He didn't say anything right away. She stared at him and he stared back. He didn't look angry about the verbal blow, though. He seemed to be considering her. Finally she couldn't stand it anymore.

"What are you thinking?"

"I'm thinking we'll find a way." He spoke softly, but his words were clear.

"A real way? A solution, not a dream that won't come true?"

He pulled his leather notebook out of his pocket and his fountain pen was suddenly in his hand. He started to write, his hand moving fast as he scribbled one-word thoughts on the page. "You said you want your mom's spirit to live on. So what does that mean?"

"The people who get the wishes—they'll know she inspired the donors."

He didn't look up from the notebook, but prompted her. "Right. But think bigger. Remember when we talked to your mom about registering for real gifts and she told us there were no limits because people get sappy and sentimental about weddings and spend too much money on candlesticks and saltshakers."

"But we didn't want saltshakers."

"Which made her mad until she thought of the Registry."

"Right. Cooper, I know all this. What are you thinking?"

"Why stop with our wedding? I mean, we're inviting a couple hundred people and that's a couple hundred wishes, but what if your mom's spirit carried on independent of our wedding."

"You mean, a permanent Wish Registry? Open it up to other brides?"

Cooper made one last note and capped his pen. He turned the notebook so Jorie could see the words he'd written across the top of the page. "The Chelsea Burke Wish Registry."

"That's brilliant!"

Her mom would have wanted to kiss him. Miriam, who kissed people as often as she handed them tissues, was definitely not going to let him out of the office again today without laying one on him. Jorie wanted to kiss him, but he had turned the notebook back around to write something else.

Look now, Mom, she thought. *He's doing it again.*

When Cooper led with his heart, he was unstoppable.

Jorie put her hand on the back of his neck to pull him down to her. "You're amazing." She opened her mouth and took his lips, needing to tell him just how wonderful he was, wanting to be closer to him so he'd know how she felt. He fumbled with his pocket, putting the notebook away, and then she was folded into his arms and they were making out in the parking lot of the Wish Team.

Maybe this was a sign that she wasn't making a mistake in giving them another chance.

When they got back inside, Miriam tidied away her used tissues while they explained their idea. Miriam would investigate whether she could set up a new registry in Chelsea's memory, one that would start accepting gifts as soon as possible. They would send out their notice asking the wedding guests who'd already signed up to fulfill their wish to pledge through the new registry. Cooper was positive his mom and dad would be able to scare up a donation or even some grant money to get the project properly launched. Jorie would reach out to business owners she knew in the bridal industry to spread the word. If Miriam wanted help designing a promotional campaign, Jorie would be more than happy to come in and help.

Miriam not only kissed Cooper, she kissed Jorie. All in all, it felt like a perfect day.

BAILEY'S RESIGNATION WAS over almost before Cooper registered that it had started. His brother stood on the steps of the Capitol and spoke the words Cooper had written. How many times had he witnessed this very same scene over the years?

There were some differences, of course. The press crowd was much bigger than normal, even by Bailey's standards. Jill was front and center behind him, but she wasn't smiling. Cooper thought she must have practiced her expression because she managed to look terribly sorry, terribly stricken, and terribly beautiful all at the same time. She even shed a few tears although not enough to mar her makeup.

It had been decided that his mom and dad wouldn't come. The few hints they'd gotten from the governor's office said he was getting push back from some of the party folks about nepotism. The

Murphys were powerful and they had enemies. Better to keep Nolan and Rachel out of sight today. Theo wasn't mentioned at all.

Jorie wasn't there either. Not that she'd ever attended a political speech before, but in the past two days, he'd gotten used to thinking about her as part of his team. He missed her.

It was late when they finally finished all of the meetings and memos and sound bites and his dad agreed they could knock off for the night. Bailey called a cab and he and Theo stood in the front hall, waiting for it to arrive. Nolan had told Bailey he had to avoid Deb's place entirely for the next couple days, until the appointment came through for Cooper.

He should head home with them. He had a million things to do tomorrow, but he couldn't make himself go.

"I'll see you guys tomorrow," he said.

"Please tell me you're not going back to the office," Theo said.

"What do you care if he's a workaholic?" Bailey asked.

"He's making me look bad," Theo complained.

"I'm not going to the office," Cooper said, hoping to cut off the discussion. "I'm going to walk."

"It's a forty-minute walk back to your place," Theo said.

"I'm not going back to my place," Cooper answered as he went out the door. The cab pulled up and his brother and cousin followed him outside.

"Going to see Jorie?" Bailey asked.

Cooper nodded.

"How is she doing?"

"Good. Really good."

The cab pulled away and Cooper headed in the opposite direction. It had been a long day and the only thing he wanted to do was find Jorie and talk to her. Somehow in the past two days, he'd found himself turning to her. For the first time ever, he had someone in the family business who was entirely on his side and he liked it.

SHE WATCHED THE RESIGNATION on TV, and even though the cameras stayed focused on Bailey most of the time, Jorie was constantly on edge waiting for them to pan out so she could see Cooper. He stood behind Bailey and off to one side, the wind stroking through his brown hair, tousling it. The speech was good. Bailey sounded strong but penitent. She left the news on while she straightened up and dusted. She avoided her office. She hadn't had a call in days and she suspected the Richfords were telling their story all over town. There was money left in her checking account for now, though, and she hadn't been able to force herself to pick up the phone or head onto Facebook or do one single bit of promotion for herself.

The pundits and announcers were not shocked by Bailey's speech. There'd been rumors for a few days and it took more than a mostly discreet affair, a resignation and a pending divorce to shock Washington. Mostly they were dissecting the speech, looking for clues about his successor. Governor Karloski's office released a statement saying it was working on the appointment.

Cooper's name came up over and over. She liked the picture the news networks showed. He was wearing a suit, but his tie was loosened and his smile was confident. She wondered if Rachel knew where the picture came from. Maybe she could get a copy.

About thirty minutes into the coverage her name was mentioned. The announcer called her a Washington business owner and daughter of the recently deceased socialite Chelsea Burke. They ran a picture of her mom with Curtis, the guy who'd wanted to send Jorie to boarding school, and she clicked off the TV. She needed some things for breakfast and it would do her good to get out for a while. She put her cell in her pocket. She wasn't expecting Cooper to call, but he might.

SHE DIDN'T NOTICE THE MAN, but he must have seen her when she was in the corner market a few blocks from her house. She had her small string bag loaded and was on her way back to her apartment when she registered the sound of footsteps behind her. At first she didn't care because it wasn't that late and a lot of folks were usually out in her neighborhood. But then a man's voice called to her, "Aren't you Jorie Burke?"

At first she thought it might be a reporter and she kept walking, remembering Nolan's bullet points. No Comment was her only reply.

"Hey, I'm talking to you. I saw you on TV. You're that prick Murphy's girlfriend, right?" He sounded drunk and angry.

Oh, God, she thought. That's not a reporter. She instantly picked up her pace and assessed her surroundings, hoping to see someone else walking nearby. But she was still two blocks from her house and there wasn't a single soul in sight. Except the one behind her.

"Stupid damn government's running this country into the ground. Entitled pricks like Murphy sitting up there like fat cats, licking the cream." He was starting to shout now and there was no doubt in her mind he was drunk. If she made it one more block, she could sprint to her house. "You got any cream for me, Jorie Burke? Or you saving it all for Murphy?"

She fumbled in her pocket for her phone and

pressed the panic button that was programmed to connect to the 911 system. "I'm calling the police," she said in a clear voice, even as she kept walking. "They'll be here any second."

"You don't need the police. We're just talking here."

She was less than a block from home now. The operator answered and Jorie started to give her information, but the man suddenly raced up and knocked the phone out of her hand. He lunged toward her again and she got her foot between his legs and kicked up as hard as she could. She connected and he crumpled to the ground.

Jorie started to scream. She darted around the parked car next to her and ran as fast as she could down the middle of the street. The guy was behind her, shouting again, but he wasn't keeping pace. She got to her place and was up the stairs before he reached her. She had her key out but then the door opened and Cooper was framed in the entry. She'd never seen anything so welcome in her life.

"What the hell?" he said.

She scrambled past him and tried to tug his arm to make him come inside.

"Cooper, he's nuts," she said. The guy yelled again. He was standing at the bottom of the steps for now, but she didn't trust he'd stay there. "He's crazy. Shut the door and let the cops handle it."

"Stay inside," Cooper said as he stepped outside and pulled the door closed. His voice was muffled by the wood when he said, "Lock the door, Jorie."

She stood frozen in place. She expected to hear shouting, but Cooper surprised her. He must have been on the top step, right outside the door, because she could hear him. His voice was controlled but commanding.

"Turn around and get off my property immediately." He wasn't negotiating, but she admired him so much at that moment because he tried to talk first. He believed in words and would always start there.

"Well, if it isn't the prick himself," the man said. "I want your girlfriend to come back out here. She freaking kicked me."

"You say one more word about her and I'm coming down there." A pause. "I'm not telling you again to get off my property."

She heard sirens, faint, but growing louder. *Please hurry, please hurry,* she thought.

"She needs to learn some manners," the guy said. "Slut."

There was a scrambling sound, a crash, and then some heavy thumps. She wrenched the door open and saw the man on the ground, Cooper was on top of him, one knee in the small of his back, his forearm braced across his neck.

The police pulled up and two officers slammed out of the first car, yelling at Cooper to back up.

He did, raising his hands and straightening in one smooth motion. His hair was disheveled and the sleeve of his dress shirt was torn half off. The man on the ground spat and started to struggle to his feet.

One of the cops moved in and tried to handcuff the guy, but he bucked up, cracking the officer's forehead with a sickening noise. Before he could get away, the other officer had taken him down from behind and wrestled him into the handcuffs.

Cooper had backed all the way to the side of her building. He kept his hands in front of him while he tried to explain, but the cop turned him around and cuffed him too.

"Cooper," Jorie said, his name slipping out. He looked up at her. Jorie felt cold. She didn't cry, but her eyes felt hot and her mouth was dry as she thought about being alone on the street with that horrible man, and then Cooper confronting him with nothing but his bare hands.

"You the one who called us?" the officer who'd stayed near the car asked her. "Can you tell us what happened?"

She came down the steps and stopped beside Cooper. He had a cut high on one cheekbone and the skin underneath was puffy. What if the guy had

had a gun, she thought. He could have been killed. "What the hell were you thinking going outside like that? You're a speechwriter, Cooper, not a freaking Navy SEAL."

He shook his head. "Someone had to shut him up," he said.

The cop cleared his throat. "I'm going to need to get statements from all of you."

The first press van pulled up before they took the handcuffs off Cooper. A bored-looking reporter climbed out and walked toward the first police officer, who was watching their attacker as he sat on the curb.

"Jorie," Cooper said in a loud whisper. "Call my dad. Right now. Go in the house and don't come out."

"I need her statement," the police officer said.

"Get it inside, or keep that reporter away from here. Quick, buddy."

But it was too late. The camera operator had filmed the whole scene while the reporter was still standing at the curb. When she panned over Cooper's face, he turned away, but not fast enough. She yelled for the reporter. "John. The guy over here in cuffs is Cooper Murphy."

"Who?"

"Bailey Murphy's little brother. The one they're talking about appointing to the Senate."

Jorie turned her back and punched Nolan's number into her phone. He answered on the first ring, and when she whispered the story to him, he started barking orders. She was to speak to no one except the police and then only in private. He would be there immediately and he'd send a lawyer to the station. There were a few other instructions, but then she heard him say, "Rachel, turn that up," and she guessed the news footage had already made it onto TV. His voice came back on the phone. "Tell them to get the freaking cuffs off him now, Jorie!"

It took a few more minutes for her to convince the police that Cooper had been protecting her and they took the handcuffs off. She managed to dab some of the dirt off his face. He shrugged out of the torn dress shirt to the T-shirt beneath. One of the reporters who'd just arrived said to her camera operator, "Get a close-up of that."

Jorie tried to block the angle, but she didn't make much of an obstacle compared to Cooper. He ignored the reporters and gave his statement. Just as he was finishing, Nolan and Rachel pulled up.

CHAPTER EIGHT

IT TOOK A WHILE, but finally the police were gone, Nolan and various other members of "the team" had finished their phone calls, and Rachel had assured herself that Cooper was physically unharmed.

Nolan had decided that far from a PR disaster, the incident was going to be gold for their team. He left with his phone glued to his ear, hoping to hear that the governor's office was ready to offer the seat to a bona fide hero.

At last Jorie and Cooper were alone in her living room. Jorie was wrapped in a blanket, curled up on one end of the couch. Cooper had paced around, but now stood leaning against the wall closest to the foyer. Jorie couldn't help thinking he was still on duty, keeping himself between her and any threats from outside.

"I'm sorry," she said quietly. "I don't have any idea what happened."

"Stop it," Cooper said. "There's nothing to be sorry about. He was drunk. End of story."

She pulled the blanket closer. "I can't believe I

didn't notice him when I was leaving the store. If I'd seen him and gone back inside where there were people around, this wouldn't have happened." She glanced at him and then quickly away. "I'm sorry I put you in that position. You didn't have to go out."

"Yeah, I did," Cooper said. He crossed the room in two quick strides, crouching on his heels in front of her. The bruise was coming up on his cheek and his hair was out of control, but all Jorie could think was how perfect he looked. "You're important to me. Nobody gets to treat you like that, especially not some scumbag who can't keep himself sober. Screw him, Jorie."

"I can't believe you were here. Thank goodness you kept your key to the place." She paused. "Why were you here?"

"I missed you. I spent the whole day on Bailey's stuff and I couldn't stop thinking that I wanted you there. When it was time to go home, I came here."

Jorie wanted that to be true. She would like to be the one he counted on the same way he was starting to be the one she counted on. Maybe she could do this. Cooper hadn't even been appointed yet and she was already anticipating what would happen once Theo won his election. That was when the charade would be over and she and Cooper would have to decide where to go from there.

HE FELT SICK TO his stomach for a long time after the cops put that guy down. Adrenaline hit him that way sometimes, but this was different. The man who had followed Jorie home was big. A tall, hefty-looking guy with muscles. Cooper couldn't stop picturing how easily he could have hurt her. He'd seen her face, the terror she felt. Somehow, seeing how vulnerable Jorie was, he finally understood a little of what she had witnessed in her mom's relationships. Not that Chelsea had been the victim of physical abuse, but she'd put herself and her daughter into the hands of one powerful man after another and they'd been let down time and again.

He got himself a Scotch, and when she asked, he poured a second one for her then sat on the couch. She scooted closer to him and he draped his arm around her shoulders.

They sat for a few minutes, not speaking, and then she looked up at him. "You want to come to bed?"

"Yes, I do," he said.

WHEN THEY GOT TO her bedroom, Jorie told him she was going to change, and slipped into the adjoining bathroom. The new nightgown she'd bought that afternoon was hanging on the back of the door. Looking at it made her tremble.

She hadn't actually bought the nightgown so much as she'd been seduced by it. She usually slept in a T-shirt and shorts and Cooper had never complained. He'd certainly never asked her to wear a negligee. The nightgown, short, sleek and silvery-blue, had been on a mannequin in the lingerie department at Nordstrom, and she'd been captivated by it. She'd immediately wondered what Cooper would think if he saw her in it. She'd promised she'd make an effort to connect with him—was this the right kind of step? If she stepped outside her comfort zone, would it bring them closer together? She'd bought it but hadn't taken the tags off yet. She hadn't expected to see him tonight, and while she was glad he was staying, she wasn't sure if she was ready to change.

She took off her clothes and then pulled the nightgown on, shivering when the fabric slid over her breasts and stomach. The tag tickled the back of her arm.

She smoothed her hands under the curve of her breasts, then down over her waist, past the hem of the nightgown to skim her thighs. Would Cooper touch her like that? Would he like this nightgown? If her usual sleeping outfit was about comfort and peaceful dreams, what was this one about? Seduction? Being a different person at night in the bedroom than she was in the light of day? Following her mother's rules for keeping a man?

Which was the cause of her confusion.

Bed was usually the place she and Cooper were most successful as a couple, but every since they'd gotten reengaged, she'd been almost dreading sleeping with him again.

Almost every single thing her mother had taught her about sex and its place in a relationship was wrong. It had taken her a long time to learn that she deserved to have as much fun as the guy she was sleeping with. That she was in charge of her contraception and health, but the guy should be just as careful about his own safety. That she didn't owe anyone anything no matter how good dinner was or how much she might be hoping for another date. That even in bed she was allowed to speak up and ask for more or different or exactly that right there but keep going for a few minutes.

She could write a book about the screwed-up lessons her mom had taught her. She'd gotten past all that eventually, and every time she enjoyed herself in bed with a good-looking guy knowing she was there free and clear with no motive other than a good time reinforced her feelings of control.

Jorie had had a good time with Cooper. But then they'd entered into this business arrangement and all of a sudden she was nervous again. What if Cooper wasn't sincere about resuming their relationship? Maybe he'd gone along with her plan just to get her back until he had the nomination sewn up. She'd asked him to be honest with her, but she had no way of knowing if he really was. All she had was trust.

Trust had never, ever been easy for her.

Stop being a chicken, she told herself. *It's embarrassing.*

But she'd been terrified before. The confrontation with the drunk had shown her in no uncertain terms that she might be strong and she might be smart, but in a physical confrontation with a man the odds of her winning were long. Cooper had taken care of her. He'd taken that guy to the ground and held him. She couldn't have done that, and she didn't like being reminded of it. Where was her power? What could she offer him that he couldn't do for himself?

She used to have answers to those questions, but that was before her business collapsed and she agreed to be an honorary Murphy political asset for the duration of the campaign.

She opened the door a crack.

He was waiting for her. He looked exhausted enough that falling asleep on his feet was a possibility. He leaned against the wall near her dresser, crystal glass dangling from one long hand, his broad shoulders filling up space in the room and in her mind. He was still wearing just his white T-shirt with his suit pants. His hair was sticking up the way it always did when he was tired. She'd teased him once that his hair had an inverse relationship to the rest of his body. As soon as he started to slump, his hair became more unruly. She loved his hair. She liked to twirl the waves in her fingers, imagining she could find patterns she'd never seen before.

With the bathroom door closed again, she put her hands on her hips, pulling the fabric tight across her waist. Her mom had never allowed herself to be bigger than a size six. Jorie hadn't been that small since puberty, but recently she'd been creeping out the top end of the tens in her closet and she was pretty sure a twelve would be nice and comfy.

Her mom had always told her that men appreciated a woman who took care of her body. She let the nightgown fall loose again, gliding over her waist and hips. If she took the nightgown off she knew she'd never put it on again. If she couldn't trust Cooper to love her the way she was, even if she was feeling vulnerable and unsure, she wouldn't ever be able to trust him.

She had to trust herself first. She wasn't wearing this nightgown just for him—the way her mom had changed her style to suit different men. Jorie was wearing it for herself—to see if she could let down her guard and meet him without all her barriers in place. She'd said she would try.

When she opened the door again, she saw that Cooper had undressed, too. He was leaning over, folding the duvet at the bottom of the bed, his black boxer briefs low and snug on his hips. Despite being close to six foot three, he was far from gangly, with lean, strong arms, gorgeous shoulders and a chest that she personally could attest to being quite delightfully firm. She'd dated a couple of athletic guys before, but Cooper was the first one who'd given her the feeling he could handle anything life threw at him. She wondered if he'd ever fought a man the way he had tonight. The muscles in his back moved as he tugged at the duvet and Jorie put her hands behind her back to stop herself from reaching for him. She felt heat in her cheeks and knew she was blushing. There was no reason for blushing—she'd seen Cooper in his boxers dozens of times. Heck, she'd seen him completely naked often enough.

But there was something different about tonight. Something intimate about being in this room with him again.

He turned and saw her and she was sure his eyes widened. Pupil dilation was probably some ancient adaptation that was useful for indicating sexual interest when the only light was coming from the flames of a fire, or in their case, the muted glow of the bulb in her bedside lamp.

You want him, she reminded herself. This is part of the plan.

She lost her nerve. She wanted to be in her shorts and T-shirt, going to bed with Cooper as usual. She'd known what she was doing when their relationship was about fun and mutual pleasure. Wearing a seductive nightgown was tantamount to declaring that she wanted him to want her. What if he didn't?

HE'D BEEN TIRED until he saw her come out of the bathroom, but then suddenly he realized what it meant when old guys in movies said, "Va va voom." She was wearing some kind of silky blue nightgown that did amazing things to her body and his.

"I want to change the sheets first," she said. She started to lift the covers off the foot of the bed. Watching her bend and stretch, the pale light from the street making enticing shadows on her skin, only made him want her more.

What the hell was going on with her? He wasn't here on a home inspection tour, he was her fiancée. Her lover. Right?

"Jorie, leave it," he said as he came around the bed and sat down in front of her.

She tugged at the sheet under him. "You're in the way."

"What's going on?" he asked.

"Nothing. I wasn't expecting you tonight but you're here and we're going to bed together so we should have clean sheets." As she talked, she continued to look anywhere but at him, shaking pillows out of their cases into a pile on the floor.

He put his hand over hers to make her stop. "I don't care about the sheets. I mean, what's going on with you?" She tried to turn away from him, but he caught her wrist. "Why won't you look at me? Are you still scared? We don't have to do this if you're scared."

She didn't answer for a second, but then she burst out, "I just feel so uncomfortable, Cooper. Like we've staged this. I can't have sex when I feel like this." She stopped abruptly.

He didn't know what she was talking about, but she was in genuine distress. Her hands were clenched so tightly he was surprised she hadn't cracked a bone, and the cords in her neck were tight as she tried to control her voice.

He leaned out and put his hands around hers. He didn't say anything, just rubbed the taut skin with his thumbs.

"You're the one who said yesterday that we should forget about everything that got us here. We're engaged and we should just enjoy it. Forget about changing the sheets. Just come to bed."

"Okay." She moved closer slowly and climbed onto the mattress. When he slid in next to her, he felt her stiffen. She moved her legs, not much, but just enough so they wouldn't touch his. He folded his arms under his head and watched her, but she didn't move, didn't roll over, didn't speak. He wasn't going to force himself on her. She'd had a serious scare, being attacked like that. On top of everything else that was going on, maybe she was just freaked out. But why was she wearing that nightgown then? She was always sexy to him, but the way her hips rose full and enticing under the silk was overwhelming. She must have known it would devastate him.

"Are you okay?"

She laughed.

"You want to talk about it?"

"The last thing I want is to talk about it."

"Okay."

"But I have to talk about it, because that's the only way this is going to work."

He raised his eyebrows. She couldn't see, but he nodded, impressed with her courage. She flopped over to face him.

He shifted and raised his arm, inviting her to move closer, to use his shoulder as a pillow. She hesitated, but then she was there, her hair silky on his bare skin, her arm across his chest.

Neither of them said anything for a few minutes.

He started to wonder if she'd forgotten that she wanted to talk. But then he felt her fingers tracing a path down his collarbone and across his chest to tease his nipple. He was almost instantly hard. He thought there was a chance she'd changed her mind and was ready to have sex, but then she started talking.

"You know what sucks?"

"No." He really didn't. Not with Jorie snuggled up in his arms, her wicked fingers teasing and stroking, and his own desire making it hard for him to think. Not much wrong with his life right at the moment.

He was supposed to be listening to her, not jumping her bones.

He could do this.

Presidents. He'd list the presidents in reverse order and maybe by the time he was finished, he'd be ready for sleep.

"We've always been good in bed," she said. "Right from our first date. But now I have this feeling that everything matters more. We're not just having fun. It's business, and I don't like it."

He tried to be subtle, but he had to move, had to press against her to relieve some of the pressure building inside him. "Yep. Sex has always been good. It is good." He must not have been as subtle as he hoped, or maybe his voice wasn't quite as controlled as he'd thought. Her fingers stopped and he added, "When we want it. When we're ready."

She relaxed again, and this time she stroked his bicep, following his arm where it lay across her hip. Who the hell had been president before Reagan? He couldn't remember.

"Carter," he muttered. "Jimmy Carter."

She sighed. Her fingers stopped stroking. Then she edged closer, pushing one thigh between his and pressing a soft kiss on his shoulder. "Maybe it will be okay," she murmured.

Warren Harding definitely hadn't been the first president, but he was damned if he could remember who'd come before him.

Forget the presidents. He kissed Jorie's forehead, right at the hairline. He'd make a catalog of her very nicest features, and maybe he'd be ready to fall asleep.

"You asked me to try to be more open, remember?"

He nodded.

"I want to do that, but it's hard. What if I...what if you..."

"What?"

"What if you don't like what you find? What if I let you in and you...and we break up again anyway?"

The hesitation in that last sentence broke his heart. He'd asked her to try without really understanding what he was asking. For a woman like Jorie who valued being in control, who didn't trust easily, who'd been hurt before, being open was a huge risk. He almost told her that they should just go to sleep—they'd both had a bad night and he was exhausted. She must be, too.

Then he thought about what might happen if they went to sleep tonight without making love. What if Jorie's fears kept compounding until she never wanted to sleep with him. How could he show her that when it came to being desirable, she already had him under her spell?

"This nightgown doesn't give you much cover, does it?"

She shook her head.

"I can see pretty much all of you."

She crossed her arms over her chest.

"You remember the other day?" he asked. "When you had those sweats on with the holes in them."

She nodded.

"I saw something down here I liked." He slid down the bed until he could move his hand up her leg, from ankle to calf, to the muscle behind her knee, and then around to the softness of her inner thigh.

She clamped her legs shut.

"Do you want me to stop?" he asked.

"No."

"You tell me, Jorie. You owe it to me and you to stop me if you're still scared or something else is wrong."

She didn't move. She didn't say stop.

He slid his hand back inside and tried to rub her skin. "I love this part of you," he murmured. "Let me kiss it."

She squeezed her legs even tighter. "You can't possibly want to kiss my thighs. I hate them."

That wasn't "stop" either.

"I love them." She'd relaxed a bit and he slid his thumb up to stroke the roll of soft flesh at the top of her thigh, right under the edge of her panty. "Especially this soft skin here."

"That's the worst part of all!" she said. "I try to pretend it doesn't exist. Leave that alone. Come up here."

He kept stroking.

"Stop?" he asked.

"Don't stop."

With his fingertips he tenderly pressed the inside of her thigh. "You know why I love this part? Because it's so soft."

She lay back on the pillows and opened her legs wider. "The softness is the problem."

"The softness is the beauty." He kissed the spot and then sucked on it, relishing the way she moved against his lips. Pressing into him. Wanting more.

"It's a very good soft. Very good." He punctuated each word with a lingering, relishing kiss. "If this was my thigh, I'd want to touch it all the time."

"They'd lock you up."

"If everyone could see you, see you like this—" He raised his head and waited until she met his eyes. "They'd understand, Jorie. You're gorgeous. Every single inch of you is beautiful. Every single hidden spot makes me want to devour you."

She blushed.

"If you'll lie there for a few minutes, I'd like the chance to show you how very little control I have when I'm near you."

She sighed and raised a forearm over her eyes. She spread her legs even farther and he knew she'd given him permission to show her what he meant. He started to peel her underwear down, sliding and stroking as he went.

When her panties were off, he positioned himself between her thighs. He wanted to show Jorie how he felt about her and he intended to take a good long time.

When she climaxed, she gripped his shoulders so hard he had to bite his lip to hold still. He waited until she stopped shuddering and then kissed his way back up her body. She pulled the nightstand drawer open and handed him a condom. When he was ready, he pulled her on top of him and she took him deep inside. She rocked back and forth, the silk of her nightgown brushing across his legs. Her breasts moved in the most delicious way and he captured them with his hands, kneading through the fabric. She pulled him up then and wrapped her legs around the back of his waist, driving him with her body. Happy to relinquish control, Cooper closed his eyes and let go.

HE'D BEEN DRIFTING in and out of a doze, but sometime around three Cooper slid out of bed and pulled out his notebook. On the page with the vows, he wrote, "I promise never to take sex with you for granted." That wasn't exactly what she'd been worried about, but it mattered. He added, "I promise to remember you're vulnerable *and* strong."

He put the book back in the pocket of his pants and then returned to bed. She shifted toward him and put her hand on his chest. He stroked her hair until she settled again.

The sun was starting to rise when he woke up the second time. He eased out from under her and went to the front door to look out at the sidewalk. There wasn't any blood, which reassured him. He'd wanted to hurt the guy last night, but now that he was calmer, he was glad he hadn't done too much damage.

He took out his notebook again and read the

promises he'd written so far. "I will always protect you as best I can," he wrote. That was getting closer to a vow.

CHAPTER NINE

THE NEXT MORNING, Cooper walked with Jorie to his parents' house. Rachel had asked her to stop by and Cooper had more rounds of lectures and strategizing with his dad. He'd never had his dad's full attention before and he was finding being on the front line with Nolan more difficult than he'd realized. Cooper was chafing at the myriad ways, large and small, his dad was trying to control his life. Bailey's escape was making more and more sense to him.

Alice's was on the way so they stopped for a bag of muffins and coffee. The Help Wanted sign was still in the window.

There was a line of people and when they saw Cooper they started to clap. One guy gave him a high five. "Good to see the government is tough on crime, right, Murphy?"

Eliot was working the register and Alice looked frazzled even though it was only eight o'clock. She must have noticed their confusion because she said,

"The story has been all over the news. Are you both okay?"

"We're just fine," Cooper said. He looked embarrassed and a slight flush joined the bruise on his cheeks.

"As soon as this crowd clears, I'm coming over to give you both a big hug, so get prepared," she said.

When it was their turn at the counter, Alice, true to her word, gave Cooper and then Jorie big bear hugs. She filled a bag with assorted muffins and made their coffee.

"You know I'd be more than happy to help you out today, Alice," Jorie said. "I have a meeting at nine, but I'll be free the rest of the morning and all afternoon."

"Oh my goodness," her friend said. "That's amazing. Come anytime."

They moved to the register where Eliot rang up their two coffees and a dozen muffins. "That's three dollars and eighty-two cents," he said.

"You sure you got everything?" Cooper asked.

"No," Eliot sighed. "Probably not." He voided the sale and started again. Alice rolled her eyes behind his back.

"Come as early as you like and stay as long as you like—if you know how to use a register, I'll pay you a bonus."

"I'm an experienced cashier, my friend," Jorie said. "I can even change the receipt roll."

"I'll have a cake here with your name on it this afternoon!"

Back outside, Cooper took a chocolate-chip muffin out of the bag and started to eat it. "That was awkward."

"You're a hero, Coop. Get used to it."

"That's nice of you to help Alice out."

"Well, I can use the money, too."

"Still no contracts?"

She shook her head, hoping to discourage the conversation. She hadn't done anything to pursue a contract and she wasn't sure when, if ever, she was going to look again. For now, working with Alice seemed like a perfect way to stave off the poor house.

"I could lend you some money," Cooper said quietly.

"Absolutely not," she answered.

"I knew you were going to say that."

"Then why did you ask?"

"Because if I didn't, I'd be the world's biggest jerk."

"So what does it make me if I refuse?"

He took her hand. "Jorie. You're always Jorie."

RACHEL WAS WAITING for them by the front door. When Cooper came in, she touched his bruise, making him wince, and then hugged him hard. "I hope Jorie yelled at you for taking stupid risks."

"Yes, Mom."

Rachel winked at her over his shoulder. "Good."

"I'm going to borrow Jorie for a few minutes, if you don't mind," she said, and then led Jorie into her office, which was in a former sun porch off the back of the living room. The office was another example of Rachel's special blend of romance and professional power. One wall was occupied by six large computer monitors and TV screens, but the desk was shiny white wood with silver trim. The bookcases were also painted white and the interior was lined with a floral paper. Instead of an ordinary ceiling fixture, a small chandelier, painted white and dangling ropes of crystals, was centered over the desk.

It was a room Jorie loved.

"Come right in," Rachel said. "How are you? Still shaken up?"

"I feel fine. I brought muffins. Cooper said you like lemon."

Rachel thanked her for the treat. "I already had breakfast, but I'll keep this for lunch."

Jorie wasn't sure why she was there.

"Did you watch Bailey's speech?"

"He did a good job," Jorie said.

"Cooper did, too."

Jorie nodded and wondered if Rachel had really asked her here for small talk.

Rachel perched on the edge of her desk and aimed a remote at the monitor wall. When she had turned on all six monitors, the combined chatter from the screens was loud, but not unbearable. She beckoned Jorie close.

"I don't want anyone else to hear what we're discussing."

Jorie nodded again.

"I met your mom over jewelry, did you know that? She complimented my necklace?"

"I remember the story."

"Well, after she found out I had a son who was single, she pumped me for information on Cooper. She was an expert at interrogation."

"She was a bit relentless," Jorie agreed.

"I admired her. I didn't know her well, then, of course, but her life fascinated me."

"She certainly kept things interesting," Jorie said. "I think when my dad died so young she got scared. She spent the rest of her life trying to find the security she'd had with him."

"But she took care of you. Somehow she always found a way to keep going," Rachel said. "I think I gave Cooper your number half in the hopes we'd see your mom again, too."

"She was very happy to have you as a friend in her last few months."

"Yes, well, I'm happy the Wish Registry is getting sorted out."

"Miriam is working wonders."

This was the conversation Rachel didn't want overheard?

When that thread petered out, Rachel bit her lip. Whatever it was she was trying to spit out was hard for her to do. Jorie wondered if she might just give up, since she didn't seem to be getting anywhere with the discussion.

Cooper's mom seemed to reach the same conclusion. She dusted her hands together.

"I have something for you." Rachel opened a cabinet in the base of the bookcase and pulled out two shopping bags. Jorie inched closer, wondering what could be inside. Something for the Wish Registry, maybe?

No. The bags were full of baby things. Cuddly blankets. Tiny leather booties. Board books and pastel sweaters. She checked the outside of the bags and saw the logos of two exclusive children's boutiques.

"Go ahead, take a look."

Jorie reached into the first bag and pulled out an exquisite hand-knit sweater and a cunning little matching cap with pompoms stitched around the rim. Under that she found a yellow and white check blanket and a stuffed bear with the softest fur she'd ever felt.

"They're beautiful, Rachel," Jorie said. "But I'm not…I'm not pregnant."

"Oh, of course not. Not now." She reached into the second bag and showed Jorie the stack of board books and the leather shoes. There was also a small wooden train with cars in the shape of alphabet letters spelling Murphy. "Bailey would have loved that. He was crazy about trains."

When she said his name, there was a tiny hitch, just a small stumble in her breathing that showed how much she was thinking about her son and how worried she was.

Jorie thought she understood why Rachel wanted her to have this baby stuff right now.

"So, if I had a friend or knew someone who was pregnant, it would be okay if I offered her these things first? She could use them for her baby while I wait to get pregnant with mine."

"What a brilliant idea," Rachel said with a beaming smile. "If you know someone, please feel free to share."

Jorie wondered if Deb would accept these gifts from Rachel. She hoped so. She didn't know Bailey's girlfriend, of course, but she couldn't imagine that she wouldn't be at least a little touched by the gesture.

Rachel shook out the yellow-and-white blanket and then refolded it, tucking the tag inside and smoothing the corners until they squared up. Watching her, Jorie understood for the first time that the baby Deb was carrying was a little Murphy—Rachel's grandchild.

She didn't have any idea what to say. All she knew was that this strong and proud woman was in pain.

"Are you going to talk to him sometime?" Jorie asked quietly.

"I can't. Not yet. Every time I see him, I want to scream at him. Not because he wanted to give up. I know how hard it can be to live a political life. It's no picnic for anyone involved, and I'd seen how much he and Jill had grown apart. But the *way* he did it—cutting us all off and putting the seat in jeopardy. Too many people have sacrificed along the way to keep that seat for the Murphys. And the cheating. That was wrong."

She was obviously not ready yet to forgive and forget. But she'd offered the gifts. She was shopping for the baby, preparing a place in her heart for him or her. She'd come around for Bailey eventually. Jorie was sure of it.

"The baby gifts will be welcome," she said.

"More than welcome, because they were chosen with love."

"Thank you, Jorie."

They repacked the bags in silence, folding the tissue carefully. When they were finished, Rachel turned the monitors back down. Confidence time was over, apparently.

"Cooper took his father to task yesterday morning, you know, over the way he treated you."

"I'm doing fine," Jorie said.

"It surprised Nolan and me. Cooper has never been the son to initiate confrontations."

"I'm sorry," Jorie said.

"I'm not," Rachel countered. "It's past time he stood up for something of his own."

They walked toward the front of the house together. Jorie put the shopping bags down in the hall outside the library and then went in to say goodbye to Cooper. He glanced up from the stack of papers he was sorting and kissed her.

"Call me," she whispered. "When you get a chance."

As she headed home, holding the bags of gifts, she wondered about Rachel. She seemed so different than Chelsea on the surface. She'd always been a part of her husband's world and was his closest confidante. She was intelligent and formidable. But this morning Jorie had seen the vulnerability.

When it came to her family, she was very much like Chelsea.

Her phone rang just as she got to her house.

"Cooper?"

"Yes."

"We need to meet your brother's girlfriend. I have something for her from your mom."

"My mom?"

"Yep. She's not ready to make up with Bailey, but I think she's already in love with the baby. Find out when we can go, okay?"

"You got it," Cooper said.

HE DIDN'T SEE HER for a few days. He got sucked into meetings and more meetings. But just because they weren't together, didn't meant she wasn't in his thoughts. The things she'd said about sleeping with him and how it felt were bothering him. He wasn't going to deny that he'd had a fantastic time, but he felt a bit guilty that they'd made love when she'd said she was feeling off.

Then, when he was in his brother's office, he'd found the perfect present for her. He was going to drop it off, no strings attached, and enjoy himself watching her open his gift.

Of course, nothing worked out the way he hoped and he was late getting to her place. He wasn't sure if she was expecting him, so he knocked quietly in case she was already in bed. He was surprised to see the light in the foyer flick on immediately. She looked out the window and then unlocked the door for him.

"I didn't want to wake you up."

"I was up," she said, but she didn't elaborate on what she'd been doing. Not watching TV, because he'd have seen the lights. He took his shoes off and left them on the mat next to the front door. She walked back into the living room, the light from the lamp picking out gold highlights in her hair. Her tank top rode up at the back and he could see the strip of pale skin just above the waistband of her shorts.

Man. He was going to have to recite the presidents again if he wasn't careful.

He trailed behind her, watching the sway of her hips and wishing he knew how to draw. He'd ask her to be his model and spend all day every day sketching the lines of her body. The desk lamp was on in the small alcove off the living room that she used as an office. She must have been working on something in there because he watched her close a notebook and tuck it into the drawer of the desk.

He leaned one shoulder against the frame of the glass French doors. "I got you a present."

She pressed her lips together.

"You have to stop that," she said. "I told you I don't like presents."

"No," he said. "You told me presents make you nervous because people sometimes give them with ulterior motives. I don't have any motives except I like to give presents."

"Well, you wouldn't admit to an ulterior motive if you had one, would you?"

"I want to watch you open this gift. Period."

He took the package from under his arm and held it out to her. He didn't have wrapping paper, but he'd improvised with a map of Allegheny County. It was a little wrinkled, but colorful enough. Who the hell didn't like presents?

"Come on, Jorie, take the gift."

It was a book. She could tell that as soon as she held the package. Not that she cared what it was because she was mad at him for forcing her to take it. He always had an ulterior motive and this time he was making a romantic gesture that would fool her into thinking they had a real relationship.

She used her thumbnail to slit the piece of tape and the paper fell away from the book.

Oh.

Oh, oh, oh. Oh.

It was a copy of her favorite edition of *Paul Revere's Ride.*

She let the paper fall to the floor as she traced

the title with her finger. The cover illustration was beautiful. Haunting and stirring. A glimpse of the horse's mane and one wild eye. Paul Revere was drawn as a square-shouldered, dark-haired man, bent over the horse's neck with one hand raised, his mouth open as he cried the alarm.

She knew Longfellow's poem wasn't historically accurate, but she'd fallen in love with the myth and this particular edition of the book when she was six, years before she'd studied history seriously and learned the real facts as they were accepted by scholars. When it came to Paul Revere, there were things she knew with her brain and things she felt with her soul.

This particular edition with its stirring watercolors belonged to her soul.

She opened to the first page and drank in the opening words. Slipshod history and a poem that sometimes forced its rhyme. She loved every bit of it. On one of their first dates, she'd dragged him to see the copy in the Smithsonian. That was back before things got complicated—when she was just flying high because she'd hooked up with a guy who turned her on and kept her laughing. A guy who had spent summers working as a tour guide in the Capitol building and wasn't bored by her idea of a fun Saturday at the museum. She'd been happy with that guy.

He came to stand behind her, looking over her shoulder at the page. "I was pacing around Bailey's office this morning, trying not to kill my dad, and it was there, on his bookshelf. I never noticed it before. He got it as a gift from one of his old professors."

"It's beautiful. I can't believe he'd let you take it. Doesn't he want it?"

Cooper shook his head. "He wants you to have it. Honest."

She didn't know what to say. How could she thank him or Bailey for this?

"The last time I held this book I was five." She glanced up at him. "I told you I stole it, right?"

He laughed. "You stole a book?"

"I can't believe I never told you this story. It was a huge scandal. We were living in Chicago and I had just started kindergarten in this super exclusive private school. I found this book in the library and checked it out, but no one told me about renewing things. I had it in my mind that I could only take it out once. The day I had to return it, I was standing there in the library and I couldn't bear to give it up."

"You poor kid. You've got the best book ever in your hands and you're thinking you have to give it back?"

"And I'd never see it again."

"So you stole it."

"Tucked my shirt into my underpants and stuffed the book down the front of my jumper."

Cooper eyed the book. "I'm trying to picture how you hid it there. It's kind of big and you were... five?"

"That was how I got caught. The teacher noticed that I suddenly looked like a box."

"Did they call the cops?"

"Just my mom. I was mortified. I was sent to the principal's office and everyone lectured me. It was awful."

"You still love the book, though?"

"Once they explained renewals to me, I took it out twenty-five times. I used to pretend it was mine." She turned to the last illustration. It showed Paul Revere walking home with his arm over his horse's neck. They were both draped in an American flag. The artist hadn't been so big on historical accuracy in his illustrations, but he knew how to make her heart beat faster. "When we moved, I think I missed the book more than anything else."

Cooper put his hands on her shoulders, kneading with gentle pressure. Then he lifted her hair and kissed the side of her neck under her ear, sending shivers down into her spine.

"You want to read me a bedtime story?" he whispered.

THEY GOT READY FOR bed and then lay down together. She skipped the fancy nightgown and just wore her usual shorts. He propped pillows behind his back and she put her head in the crook of his shoulder. He kept his arm around her while she read. He stroked her hair and her shoulder, but that was it. When she finished, she propped the book up on her nightstand so she'd see the cover as soon as she woke up and turned out the light. She lay back down and squirmed until her backside was resting against him and she could slide one leg between his.

"Good night, Jorie," he said.

She patted his shoulder and then there was quiet. Jorie thought he'd fallen asleep until a few seconds later when she shifted positions to get closer to him. "Taft."

"What did you say?" she asked.

"Nothing," he said. "Trust me. It was nothing."

CHAPTER TEN

WORKING FOR ALICE wasn't the easiest thing Jorie had ever done. Her friend had built her bakery's reputation on hard work, skill and a devotion to customer service that was almost pathological. Eliot's issues with the register and price chart were forgiven because he was perfection itself when difficult customers needed something.

Jorie did her best, but she had to admit the only part of the bakery business that really got her fired up was the packaging. Alice had fifteen different adorable boxes and matching bags to suit all sorts of baked goods. Jorie's favorite was the tray that held six cupcakes in individual boxes. Each Lucky's package could be tied with string dispensed from an elegantly simple machine.

Jorie enjoyed placing crystallized violets on the cake Alice had made for a bridge club luncheon, and Eliot turned out to be surprisingly funny.

Alice was grateful she was there and she chatted up Jorie's wedding planning business to every customer who looked even remotely like a candidate.

Jorie couldn't remember the number of times she'd had to shake someone's hand while Alice listed her many virtues. This quest to revitalize her business was exasperating. And humiliating. And so sweetly supportive that Jorie couldn't disappoint Alice by telling her to forget it. She hadn't gotten any appointments out of her efforts, but she supposed it was hard to imagine the woman making change in the bakery as a wedding planner.

Everything would have been just fine if she weren't so completely, bone-wearingly bored. During the lull after lunch and before Eliot had to leave for history class, she ducked into the back where Alice was setting up for a cake tasting that evening. She felt a stab of envy. Alice's business was thriving enough that she could afford to hire and retain extra counter helpers, even if one half of them was incompetent.

"Who's the bride?" she asked.

Alice handed her a menu card.

"Grace Blackwell? You're doing Grace Blackwell's wedding?"

"Fingers crossed. She hasn't signed the contract yet."

"Man, I wanted that wedding." Jorie took another look at the card. "Is she really doing pink and powder-blue as her colors? What is it, a baby shower theme?"

"Don't be mean."

Jorie slumped into one of the white chairs. She wondered if it was the same chair she'd been sitting in when Cooper broke up with her. "Have you ever had anyone else get dumped during their cake tasting? Or was I the first?"

"The first in the bakery, but I've lost commissions because the wedding got called off. You have, too, I'm sure."

"Remember the Garvin-Houston fiasco? What was that whack doodle's name? Felicia, right? Remember when she told us her monogram was *F-G-H,* alphabetical order!" She made her voice rise at the end, the same way FGH's voice always did. Sharp and shrill.

The bride and groom had requested an intimate setting where they could hold the ceremony and the reception without having to travel between locations. A nice plan, until FGH and the best man took off in one of the wedding limos while the groom waited at the front of the room with the justice of the peace. Mrs. Garvin-Houston dumped an entire bowl of shrimp over the head of the groom's mom. Punches were thrown. Dresses ripped. The cake got knocked over and trampled. Jorie slipped on the icing and tore the knee out of her favorite black pants. Nobody got their deposit back for that one.

"Yeah, that was quite a night."

She handed Grace's menu card back to Alice. "I wanted to do Grace Blackwell's wedding and I couldn't even get a callback. If I had a contract like that, I'd be back in business."

Alice dropped the card on the table. "I can talk to her. You want an interview?"

"She signed with Something Blue at least two months ago. She's not going to talk to me now."

If Alice had had a skinny black mustache, she'd have twirled the ends. "First of all, she needs to fire whomever she hired because those colors are hideous, and second, I can guarantee she'll talk to you if I ask her."

"What? Why?"

"When we were about twenty, we went to Los Angeles together for a few months. Grace did a very bad thing with a very bad man. She does not want anyone to find out about this bad thing or this bad man. Between you and me, she thinks I have a picture, which I don't." Alice smoothed the menu card on the table. "She's always extremely accommodating to me."

Alice pulled out her cell and made the call. Sure enough, Grace said she'd like nothing better than to meet Alice's friend, the wedding planner.

Jorie went home about an hour before Grace was supposed to arrive at Alice's for the meeting. She opened the French doors to her office and sat at her desk for the first time in days. The plans for the *Rebel Without a Cause* wedding were still tacked on her inspiration wall. If she got Grace Blackwell to hire her, she'd be back in business.

Ace this one meeting and she could be up to her neck in wedding details. Brides and flowers and all the things that went into making one dream day.

Wedding planning was something she knew how to do. It wasn't just her taste and creativity. She could read the deep wishes underlying a couple's conversation.

She didn't have enough time to do a full treatment the way she would have for a regular client meeting, so when she followed Alice into the tasting room that evening, she had the quick and dirty three-page binder she'd pulled together. It was pretty good considering how little time they'd had, and there wasn't a hint of pink or powder-blue anywhere.

Grace, a tall, thin woman with a long face and fashionably straight blond hair, was talking to Alice.

They stopped when they saw Jorie, but not before she heard the words "James Dean." *Perfect.* Her fame preceded her.

Grace scanned Jorie from head to toe. "So you're Jorie, huh? I've heard about you. Nadine Richford said you suggested a war theme for her wedding."

Jorie choked. "She misunderstood."

Alice stepped in quickly before she could explain further. "Not everyone gets Jorie's concepts, Grace. She's very avant-garde."

"You know how it is when you're making art," Jorie said. Alice had told her to be sure to praise Grace's "career" in three low-budget films and one straight-to-video slasher flick.

Grace nodded. "Nadine has very pedestrian taste. She wore a pearl choker in her engagement photo."

Right then Jorie started to see the concept. Grace would want something utterly original, something on the cutting edge that also was traditional enough to keep her front and center. Maybe steampunk—the modernist twist on Victorian styling that was so popular in graphic novels right now. She bet Grace would love it if her theme was a little challenging. She'd relish the chance to explain her complicated and artsy self to her friends and family.

Jorie knew what she needed to say next. She'd have to walk a careful line between enticement and flattery, but she could tell that Grace was ripe for the picking. If she followed this conversation through, she had a great chance of signing a contract for a huge, well-funded wedding. The drawback was that she'd have to spend the next year with Grace Blackwell talking over every detail of her wedding, and in the end, what would she have? A gorgeous celebration, the perfect day. That was what Jorie was selling, what she'd always sold.

And then what? After the perfect day, what would her clients have? Was she contributing to the illusion that people could make a perfect marriage if they had the perfect wedding?

She knew what she was supposed to do, but she couldn't make herself say the words that would lead to the deal. "Um, Grace? It was great to meet you, but I have another appointment."

"Wait, what?" Alice gave her an are-you-insane look.

"I thought we were going to talk about my wedding," Grace protested.

Jorie patted her shoulder. "You should ditch Something Blue. That's my advice. If you go with them, your wedding is going to be insipid. Like vanilla pudding. Like something Nadine would like. Call Aria Hall and ask her about steampunk. She can pull it off, and I guarantee you won't see a hint of powder-blue all day."

"But you don't have to call Aria when you have Jorie. You could do a killer steampunk wedding for Grace, since it was your idea. Right, Jorie?"

Alice was trying so hard for her and Jorie just wanted to let it all drop.

"You know what would really make your wedding stand out?" Jorie asked. "If you did a Wish Registry."

"I heard about yours, but doesn't that mean you don't get presents?"

"You can do half and half, or a limited number of wishes. It's up to you. What you do get is good press. I guarantee if you fill a couple of wishes through your wedding registry, you'll get your picture taken."

"I'm intrigued," Grace said.

Jorie recited Miriam's phone number while Grace put it into her phone. Then she headed out the back door to the street. Alice came out a few seconds later.

"What just happened?" she asked.

"I'm not sure," Jorie said. "Can we not talk about it? I really do have to go, Alice, but thank you. Thank you so much for setting that meeting up and for caring enough about me to keep trying to find clients and for being here with me."

Alice shrugged. "It wasn't that big a deal. I love it when I can mention L.A. to Grace. She's so bitchy to everyone—it's good if I remind her that she's vulnerable."

"I'll see you tomorrow, okay?"

COOPER WAS AT HER PLACE when she got there. He'd started stopping by every evening when he finished with his dad. She said hello, but went right past him into her office.

"What's going on? You get a contract?"

"No," she said. "Alice got me a meeting with a client and it was all going great and then I realized I had to get out of there before I took the job."

"What?"

"I don't like weddings anymore. I'm not sure I ever really did."

He hovered in the doorway.

"You know why I became a wedding planner?" She grabbed a stack of boxes off the shelf and piled them near the door. A white wire basket filled with fabric swatches from linens she used at showers was next.

Cooper shrugged. "I assumed you liked weddings."

"No. My mom liked weddings. She loved weddings. As you know. After college, I was in Arizona staying with her and Marie at the spa. I didn't have a job yet and I really didn't want to take out the loans I'd need for grad school. But I was signed up for the LSAT and the GRE. I just needed a little time to figure things out. While I was there, Marie had a couple come in who wanted to do a destination his-and-hers bachelor-party thing. Marie asked my mom and me to help plan it. By the time the date for the GRE came around, I had a wedding booked and Marie made me a set of business cards."

She opened the cupboard beneath the bookcase next to the windowsill. The shelves were tightly packed with photo boxes where she stored a lot of her ideas. She wiggled the top box, trying to pull it out, and when it finally popped free, she sat down hard on her tailbone. "Damn it!"

Cooper came into the room and sat next to her. The contents of the box, labeled and color-coded index cards on which she'd glued or stapled photos, swatches, even paint samples, were scattered in front of them on the floor. He carefully pulled them back into a pile and started straightening them.

"Stop," she said. "I'm going to get a garbage bag."

"Jorie," Cooper said quietly. "What's going on?"

"I don't want this anymore. I don't want any of it. I don't want this to be my life." She held up a card showing a bouquet of calla lilies.

"But you're good at it," he said. "Don't sell your-self short."

"I don't want to be good at it. I want..." She sighed. "I want something else."

"What?"

She stood up and used her foot to slide the empty

box and stacks of spilled cards under the desk. She'd come back later and clean up.

"Something that lasts," she said. "I've been in business nine years," she told Cooper. "In the beginning I was scraping by, but then I got established and I could pick and choose my commissions." She stretched to open the bottom drawer of her desk and pulled out a binder, which she dropped in his lap. "These are my records—one for every wedding. It's fifty-four couples."

"That's a lot of happy people. People you helped. People who have wonderful memories because of you."

"Happy couples? Want to bet?" She sat at the desk and turned her computer on. "The records are public, you know. You can see exactly how long a marriage lasts because it's all recorded nice and neat at the courthouse. Give me a name."

He started flipping through the binder. Each couple had a page. Their names and a photo were at the top, along with the date of the wedding and any of the other parties she coordinated for them, including showers and the rehearsal. Some people let her plan their bachelorette parties. She kept a database of wedding party members because it was so much easier to pick up a contract from someone who'd seen her work before. She called them legacies.

"Celine Marsh," Cooper said.

"I remember her. She invited six-hundred and seventy people for the Case Mansion, which has a strict limit of four hundred. Luckily, either she wasn't very well-liked or a lot of her friends and family were invited to a competing event because she ended up with a little over three hundred guests. She was furious, but I kissed every single *No* reply that came in."

Cooper was smiling. The story was funny—now. It had been terrifying at the time, but she'd learned a huge lesson about how to keep control.

The search results were on the screen. "Divorced before the year was up."

He turned the page. "Fiona Dempsey-Foley."

She already knew the answer to that inquiry. "That wedding was beautiful. She was a step dancer and wanted this embroidered plaid fabric at the reception. I thought it wouldn't work, but we made table runners that the guests loved. She saved them. Said she was going to use them at the christening when they had their first kid. She cheated on him, I heard. Their marriage was annulled, but at least it was before they had a baby."

She leaned down and turned the page. "These guys are still together. For now."

Another page. "Divorce. Divorce. Together." She flipped faster through the book, her entire career flying by in bright colors.

"What are you doing, Jorie?"

She snapped the binder shut. "I did fifty-four weddings in nine years and close to half of the couples are already divorced."

"You're not a marriage counselor, Jorie. You're a wedding planner."

"But is this what I'm going to spend my life doing? Working with these people, giving them a dream day when maybe they shouldn't be getting married at all? I mean, people called me the wedding whisperer. It's because I get it. I get them wanting that perfect day because my mom wanted it so much."

"You give them a gift," he said. "You can't predict what will happen later."

"I don't have to predict. I know what will happen later. They track divorce statistics. It's not like these numbers are a surprise."

"So what are you saying?"

"I don't want to devote myself to *moments*, Coop. I want to do something that matters." Jorie dropped the binder into a bucket of silk flowers and ribbon samples. "I want something real."

She spent the rest of the evening emptying her office. Cooper offered to help, but she told him it was something she'd rather do herself. She salvaged what she could to donate to charity and the rest went into green garbage bags or recycling. When she was finished, the office was completely empty, every shelf had been wiped down and the wood surfaces polished. She could go in there tomorrow and start a new business or she could see about moving a chair and a lamp in and creating a reading nook. Whatever she wanted, the space was hers again. She just had to fill it.

"HEY, JORIE." Theo opened the door to Cooper's apartment and let her in. "You ready for Operation Meet the Family?"

She set the shopping bags down inside the door. "What?"

"Cooper said we're not allowed to talk about the super secret meeting with Deb. He thinks his dad is more hooked in than the CIA and he's going to swoop in with the black SUVs and stop it if he finds out we're talking about it. He only agreed to let you guys go if you kept it completely off the radar."

Cooper came out of the bedroom. "You'll get chucked in the black SUV, Theo. Jorie, he'll probably just kill. She's non-essential."

"Thanks, Cooper," Jorie said.

"Hey, you're essential to me." Cooper kissed her. "But I'm not the one with the black SUVs."

Theo flopped into a recliner and spun it so he was facing the TV where a baseball game was in progress.

"Stop trying to scare Jorie. Your dad drives a Cadillac."

Cooper put his arms around her waist and pulled her in close. He kissed her again and then murmured, "He's got tinted windows, though." His lips were warm and inviting. "Very shady."

Theo turned the game up. "You won't have to worry about Nolan because the vice squad will be on your butts if you don't quit making out in public."

Cooper ran one hand through her hair as he kissed her again. "You treat this place like a hotel, but it's actually my apartment, remember, Theo?"

Theo groaned. "You could have pity on me. Your dad told me I can't date until January. You were a smart man to get engaged when you did."

Jorie stepped back. She hated being reminded of their arrangement.

"He's an idiot, you know that."

"I know," she said. "But we should go." She raised her voice. "Theo, are you ready?"

"I'm not allowed to go," he said. "Nolan's worried I'll get spotted with the sinners and tarred with the same brush."

"Well, what about you?" she asked Cooper.

"Different rules for the appointee and the candidate, Jorie," he said. "Wait one sec."

He jogged back into his bedroom, and when he

reappeared he was carrying a stuffed lamb with a pink satin ribbon around its neck.

"Is that Lamby?" Theo asked.

"Not *the* Lamby," Cooper said. "It's a brand new, clean, with working musical parts Lamby II."

"Who's Lamby?" Jorie asked.

"Cooper's only friend when he was little."

"Bite me." He held the lamb out to Jorie. "Wind it up. It plays 'Danny Boy.'"

She wound the silver handle planted in the lamb's side and, sure enough, a tiny metallic-sounding version of "Danny Boy" played. "You had a lamb like this when you were a kid?"

"I guarantee he's still got it, Jorie. You should check under his pillow."

"Mock all you want, Theo. I'm not ashamed. Bailey's kid is going to love Lamby II."

She handed the toy back to him. It looked incredibly small in his big hands, and she knew her cavewoman instincts were attracted to a good protector. She couldn't help watching as he tucked the lamb under his arm while he shrugged into his black leather jacket.

He turned to go, then said, "Whoa. Those bags have baby logos on them."

"They're the things your mom bought. I told you."

"I know. It's the bags. We have to conceal them

just in case we do get spotted." He put the lamb inside one. "I'll grab a couple garbage bags."

It only took a few minutes for them to hide the retail bags and stow them in the backseat of his Jeep. The breeze coming in through the windows as they drove ruffled the plastic bags, a reminder that nothing about this day was normal. If they wanted to visit Deb and Bailey, they should be able to. If she and Cooper wanted to bring a present to Deb—hell, if they wanted to get her a stroller and a huge stack of cloth diapers—they shouldn't have to hide it in garbage bags. She'd thought her mom was consumed with image, but the Murphys took things to an entirely new and uncomfortable level.

And then there was the way Cooper's family treated him like a second-class citizen. As if there'd been an entrance exam around the time he was born and he hadn't performed well. Got his goo's mixed up with his ga's or didn't drool with enough precision. She could see no rational explanation for why he had been passed over in favor of Theo, and she had no idea why he wasn't pissed.

"I still can't believe my mom sent all that stuff."

"It's her grandchild, Cooper. That's a huge deal."

"Not a big enough deal to start talking to Bailey again."

"Maybe that's the thing. I think she's mad at him, but she's hurt, too. He didn't trust your parents enough to ask if he could leave the Senate. He didn't give them a chance to plan. I bet if I were a mom and I found out my kid didn't trust me, my feelings would be hurt."

"I guess."

Neither of them spoke again during the ride to Lucky's. The press had staked out Deb's apartment so they'd decided they would meet in Alice's tasting room. Jorie had a built-in excuse to be there for her job and Cooper had spent enough time going in and out recently that he wouldn't be noticed. Alice had talked to the chef at the small Mexican restaurant whose back door was across the alley from hers, and Deb and Bailey were coming through that way.

Eliot was working at the counter when they opened the front door. The bakery was empty for the moment, and Jorie took her first steady breath since they'd parked the car. Maybe this would work. Eliot nodded toward the back room. "Your party arrived a few minutes ago."

Cooper hefted the garbage bags again and they headed into the tasting room.

Alice had the shutters closed so the room wasn't as bright as usual, but otherwise it was set up as if for a standard cake tasting, right down to the silver tray holding an assortment of cakes. Every element was in place to provide a cover for their meeting. Bailey was seated beside a woman with long dark hair at one of the small tables, but he stood up when he heard the door open.

"Cooper, Jorie," he said. "Meet Deb Collier."

COOPER'S FIRST THOUGHT was that he hadn't seen Bailey smile like that in years. His second thought was that his mom should be here. And then he stopped thinking and crossed the room to meet Deb and the baby she was carrying. Until she stood up and he saw the actual bump, indisputable evidence of his first niece or nephew, he hadn't totally taken in the fact that Bailey was going to be a dad soon. He dropped the bags and put his arms around both of them and kissed the top of Deb's head. "Welcome to the family."

Bailey's voice sounded strangled when he said, "I told you he's really a woman trapped in an ugly man's body."

Cooper let them go, but he didn't move away. "I've been waiting to meet her, Bay. Cut me some slack."

Deb straightened the collar of the brown jacket she was wearing over a pair of brown pants with a faint white pinstripe. "It's nice to meet you, too, Cooper," she said. And then she burst into tears.

For an instant they were all frozen. Deb grabbed a napkin off the table behind her and buried her face in it. "I'm sorry. Hormones." She sniffed, obviously trying and failing to control her tears. "I'm not normally like this."

Jorie went to her and patted her back. "It's okay."

Bailey patted her from the other side, looking completely out of his depth.

Deb lifted her head after a minute and swiped away the mascara streaked under her eyes. "I'm sorry. This has all been so stressful."

Cooper snagged a box of tissues off a small table and Deb grabbed a handful and blew her nose.

After that introduction, it seemed easy to sit down together to eat cake and get to know one another.

After a few minutes, Cooper snagged the garbage bags and carried them over to the table. "We brought you some presents."

"It's too much," Deb protested, but Bailey dove right in. He opened the first bag and found the stuffed lamb on top. He started laughing.

"Are you kidding me? You got my kid a Lamby?"

"Lamby II," Cooper said.

"You want him to get beaten up at summer camp?"

"Nobody ever beat me up," Cooper insisted. "And I only brought him to camp one year."

"You took your stuffed animal to camp?" Jorie asked.

"I was only seven. Maybe my brother should have told me to leave him home."

Deb reached for the toy and wound the handle to listen to the song. "I think it's perfect. Lamby II is most welcome, Cooper. Thanks."

Bailey dragged out one shopping bag and put it on the table while Jorie retrieved the other one. "Who's all this from if not you guys?" Bailey asked.

Cooper shrugged. "Mom."

Bailey slowly pulled his hand out of the bag. "What?"

"Mom sent it. She gave it to Jorie so we could give it to you."

"Can you excuse us?" Bailey asked Deb and Jorie. They nodded. Cooper followed him across the room and through a door into a small storage space.

"Mom's not talking to me," Bailey said. "But she's shopping for stuff for my kid?"

"It's her grandchild." Cooper didn't know what to tell his brother. He thought his mom was being crazy, but on the other hand, she was trying. "I'm taking it as a good sign."

"A sign of what?" Bailey asked.

"That she's going to come around."

"Maybe I don't want her to come around. Maybe I've learned something during these past three weeks and I don't want Mom or Dad or their particular blend of Murphy-family crazy anywhere near my child."

"You don't mean that," Cooper said.

"I might."

Cooper smacked his hand on a case of flour. "Bailey, I'm turning my life inside out to keep peace in the family. To help salvage something from the mess you made so you and Mom and Dad don't spend the rest of your lives hating each other. What the hell do you mean by saying you don't want them around?"

"I told you not to do that, Coop. I told you not to get your life tied up in theirs."

"That doesn't make sense. They're our parents. How can we not be tied up in each other?"

"You have to figure out what you want, Coop, and then go for it. Don't let this Murphy crap drag you off in some direction you never thought of, because if you do, before you know what's happening, you're going to be just as stuck as I was."

"You know what?" Cooper said. "Maybe you weren't as stuck as you thought. Maybe if you trusted Mom and Dad a little bit, you could have talked to them and found a way out that wouldn't have messed everything up."

"You don't need that, Jorie," said.

CHAPTER ELEVEN

IT WAS OBVIOUS Cooper and Bailey were arguing. Jorie tried to get Deb interested in the gifts, but as soon as she heard they were from Rachel, she'd shut down.

"Rachel is going to come around," Jorie said. "It's been a hard time for her, but she'll get over it."

"That's easy for you to say," Deb said.

"What?"

"Look at you. You're the perfect one. You have your perfect engagement, your perfect husband. Your perfect wedding and your perfect little fairy tale. The Murphys must love you because you're everything they want."

"It's not like that," Jorie said.

"Yes, it is. I'm always going to be the other woman to them. Our baby will always remind them of Bailey's resignation. There's no way we'll ever fit in. Not the way you do."

Jorie was shocked that Deb thought of her this way. That she'd somehow been presented as a Murphy insider. Had she been that good at the chameleon act again? Was she following her mom's recipe so closely that she was already seen as the perfect Murphy spouse?

"Deb, I can't speak for Rachel, but the day she gave me these gifts, she was genuinely sad. She wants to reach out. I know she will. Give her time."

"She's the one who has the power, Jorie. If she wants to be part of our lives, she can show up herself, and if she wants to cut us out of her life, she can do that, too. She already has. Bailey told me his parents don't see a boundary between family and work—his marriage was part of his job, just like yours is part of Cooper's job. You better be careful they don't turn on you, too."

Jorie didn't know how to respond. The storage room door banged open and Cooper strode out, Bailey close on his heels

"You're not leaving that stuff here, Coop."

"I'm not taking it back."

"Yes, you are. You take it back and tell Mom if she wants to give the baby a present she can do it in person."

Jorie watched Cooper gather up his temper. He tightened his jaw and took a deep breath, all the while clenching and unclenching his fists. She was so caught up watching him, she almost missed his first words.

"Bay, please. Don't do this to her."

"She made her choice."

Cooper turned to Deb. She put the sweater she'd been holding back into the shopping bag. She'd made her choice as well.

"Fine," Cooper said. He took the handles of the two bags and turned to Deb. "It was wonderful to meet you. Take care of yourself and the baby."

When they came through the swinging door into the bakery Eliot said, "How was the cake?"

"Ask my brother," Cooper snapped.

Jorie called a thank-you and followed him out. He popped the back window on his Jeep and put the presents inside before slamming it shut.

When they were both settled in their seats, he said, "I can't give that stuff back to my mom."

Jorie wanted to agree with him, but she thought he was wrong. She'd seen Rachel's face when they talked about Bailey and the baby. Rachel would make a lot of choices based on what Nolan wanted and what was best for the family's political aspirations, but Jorie didn't think she'd want this rift with Bailey to be permanent. She couldn't believe anyone would make that choice.

"You owe it to her to be honest," she said. "You have to let her make her own decision about what to do."

Cooper jammed the key into the ignition and turned it hard. "Since when do Murphys get to make choices?"

THE NEXT DAY meant three weeks had gone by and Governor Karloski still hadn't committed to appointing Cooper and thereby smoothing the way for Theo to run. Nolan decided earlier in the week that if they hadn't heard by today they would travel to Harrisburg in person. Jorie's presence wasn't necessary in the unofficial delegation, but Cooper had asked her if she'd be able to make the overnight trip.

They were planning to take four cars, including Cooper's Jeep. They were all double-parked in front of the Murphy home, trying to sort out rides and suitcases, when Nolan got a call. The governor wouldn't see them. They were to sit tight and the announcement would come when he was ready. Not a moment before.

It was a power play, plain and simple, and the Murphys were forced to wait.

Cooper's dad wasn't the kind of guy who dealt well with his plans being thwarted. Especially by Karloski, who was quickly ascending the ranks of Nolan's Least Favorite People. The shouting only lasted about ten minutes and no tires were damaged, although several were kicked.

Nolan shut himself up in his library, Theo went

to the airport to head back to his office and Bailey took off, no doubt to see Deb. Rachel came into the kitchen where Jorie and Cooper had taken refuge with coffee.

"You might as well leave, too," she said. "Your dad's not in the frame of mind to get anything done."

"What are you going to do?" Cooper asked her.

"Hide out, mostly. I have some correspondence I need to catch up on. The alumni magazine for my sorority came today. I might open that and see which of my cronies have died this year."

"Mom, that's awful."

"It's what we do, Cooper. You'll see when you're my age."

"Your age! You sound as if you're ninety-three."

Rachel swatted the back of his head. "I'm old enough, sonny boy."

Cooper laughed. "All right, I admit it, you're a geezer."

She left them alone and Jorie shrugged. "Maybe I'll head to the bakery and see if Alice needs help."

"What if we went on a date?"

As soon as he said it, he knew exactly how they should spend their day. She looked skeptical. Well, he wasn't going to nudge her. He wanted her to say yes because she wanted to.

"What?"

"I've got a surprise I'd like to show you."

"You want to show me a surprise?" She brought her coffee cup to the table and put it down. She'd brought a box of Linzer cookies from the bakery that morning and now she put one on a plate, dusting the sugar off her fingers into the sink.

She handed him the cookie and then got one for herself.

"Okay, I'll bite. What's the surprise?"

He had a mouthful of cookie so he couldn't laugh at her, but he raised his eyebrows. When he could speak, he said, "'What's the surprise?' You must know that's not a logical question. If I tell you what it is, then it's not a surprise anymore."

She nodded. "That's fair. Okay, then how do I know I'll like the surprise? I generally hate surprises."

"I know you'll like it the same way you knew I'd like red velvet cake. I know you."

"I don't like watching baseball. Not even live baseball." There was suspicion in her voice. Totally unwarranted. He didn't like watching baseball with anyone except Bailey and a few other guys who'd grown up waiting for baseball to come back to D.C. Watching with someone who didn't care was like going to a movie where you had to explain the jokes—not worth the effort.

"The Nats are on the road. But I wouldn't take you

to a baseball game, anyway. I know you wouldn't enjoy it. I also wouldn't take you to a Thai restaurant, or any place that doesn't serve cake, or to a book signing for a celebrity memoirist unless it was John Cusack."

She shook her head, but she smiled. "Fine," she said. "Show me the surprise."

"I'm going to get out of this suit and put on some jeans. Can you wait for a minute?" He was glad he had the clothes he'd packed for the road trip. He put his plate and coffee cup in the dishwasher. When he was walking past her, she looked up.

"Is it a dirty surprise?"

Just hearing her say "dirty" made his body tighten. He leaned down and kissed her neck. She was wearing a tank top under a silky shirt and he pushed her hair aside and kissed the bare skin right above her collarbone. Then, with his lips barely touching her, he whispered, "If you want a dirty surprise, I can arrange that."

A shiver ran over her skin. He put one hand on her bicep and kissed her mouth, relishing the way she kissed him back. "I know lots of things you like," he whispered. She shivered again and then tilted her head to deepen their kiss.

When he pulled away to head upstairs to change, he trailed his hand down her arm, shoulder to wrist to fingertips. She was so gorgeous. She sighed when he walked away. It made him smile.

"I THINK THIS PLACE is closed," Jorie said. The day was warm, but they were standing in an alley and the buildings on either side were tall enough that the shade was almost chilly. She crossed her arms and shivered.

"It's not closed," Cooper said. He turned the knob on the steel fire door marked "Museum" and walked inside. "Marty doesn't believe in advertising. Says if people don't care enough to find him, he doesn't want them poking through his stuff in the first place."

"What stuff?" Jorie said, looking around the shabby lobby with the worn linoleum door and a small wooden table that was bare except for a stack of brochures, a plastic doorbell affixed to the counter with duct tape, and a locked Plexiglas box labeled "Donations." A few crumpled dollar bills lay at the bottom amongst a mix of change, several green plastic army figures and a keychain with a metal horse hanging off the end. "Whatever it is, I hope he's not living off the donations."

Cooper took a twenty out of his wallet and stuffed it in the box. He hit the button on the doorbell and smiled. "Just wait."

There was a crackling noise and then a fife and

drum song filtered out of a speaker over the table. The first time he'd come here, Cooper had been on assignment. He was supposed to be writing a piece for his high school newspaper about citizen historians. His dad had gotten him appointments with two Georgetown professors who'd written books, and Cooper had dutifully interviewed them, but it was an excruciating experience. They were both about as pompous as it was possible to be. The second professor made a joke about Marty and his museum and Cooper had come here directly from the interview. The afternoon he spent at Marty's remained one of his best memories.

Jorie looked at him, and he put his arm around her shoulder. "Listen."

The music faded and Marty's speech started. Cooper had asked him one time if he'd ever had any training as an actor or even a newscaster, but the question had irritated Marty. He said when he'd been in school, everyone was taught to deliver an oral reading properly—he didn't use the word *elocution*, but he might as well have. Cooper had let him rant, but he knew there was something different about Marty's speech. Maybe it was the passion he had for the subject.

"When you read about that day, the words have the ring of history, of heroism. An assault at dawn. An army too stubborn to retreat. A cavalry charge

to save the day. Lee. A.P. Hill. Harpers Ferry. The Army of Northern Virginia. Miller's Cornfield and Dunkers Church. What the words conceal… or maybe what they illuminate…is the story of the single bloodiest day in the long and bloody history of the American military. Some call it Sharpsburg. Some call it Antietam. The name doesn't matter. What matters are the actions taken, the decisions made, the tiny flicks of fate that led two great forces into a day of crippling destruction.

Open the door and prepare to live that day with the fighting men of the American Civil War."

She was caught. He saw it in her face and knew Marty's voice had worked its magic one more time.

"Open the door."

Inside the room was dark. Emergency lighting lined a path on the floor. He waited until the door had closed behind them and then took her hand to walk forward. A weak light glowed around a button on the edge of a low table. He couldn't see her, but he felt her turn to him.

"Push the button."

The speakers crackled as the first section of the diorama lit up and then Marty's voice came on again, guiding them through the days leading up to the battle. When Marty's voiceover ended and the music trailed off, the lights faded and the next section of the path lit up, a glowing button beckoning them forward. She squeezed his hand and whispered, "You were right. I do love this."

THERE WAS NO WAY a diorama should be so heartbreaking. That was the first thing Jorie thought. Dioramas were for second-graders and Girl Scouts and model train enthusiasts. They were…cheesy. But as she followed the glowing lights through the dark room, watching as one section of battle after another was lit up, hearing the haunting voice lead her through the battle toward the victory that wasn't a victory, she forgot all of her misgivings about the diorama and immersed herself in the experience.

The room remained dark, even when small explosions lit up one section of the battlefield or the emergency lights came on to illuminate the path to the next station. She couldn't see Cooper, but it didn't really matter. She knew exactly where he was. Her hand was in his, warm and strong, his thumb occasionally stroking over hers. His fingers tightened when A.P. Hill's cavalry thundered in from Harpers Ferry and she squeezed him back. Their shared love for cavalry charges had been one of the first things she liked about him.

At the last station, he pulled her in front of him, crossing his arms over her chest and leaning his chin on her hair. He was tall enough that she felt enveloped by him, anchored by him. She should slide out of his arms, but instead she leaned back into him. In the dark room of this unique museum there was no one to see if she let go for a little while and let him be in charge. It felt good to surrender. He tightened his arms, and she let her head fall back onto his shoulder. Was this what her mom felt like when she'd found a guy and rearranged her life to fit his? When she'd left her old life behind and thrown herself entirely into his. Had she felt supported? Or had Chelsea been scared? There must have come a time when she'd been let down so often that she'd expected rejection instead of happiness, right? Or had she kept hoping, right up until the last guy, that she'd found a good one. Someone she could spend her life with, who wouldn't leave her?

The voice-over ended and lights illuminated the path to the door.

Cooper gave her a last squeeze and then started to walk out.

"Do the lights come on?" she asked.

"The door is this way," he answered, misunderstanding her question.

"No, I mean, if you stay in here, do the overhead lights come on? I want to see the whole thing."

"It's better if you don't," Cooper said. "It kind of ruins the magic."

"I'm over my disappointment about Santa Claus.
I can take it."

He pressed one hand on her shoulder. "Stay here
for a second. I know where the switch is."

He was gone and the room seemed big and empty
as she stood alone in the dark. When the lights
switched on, it took her a few seconds to adjust.

"Wow," she said.

"I know."

The room was a maze of low plywood tables
covered by thick Plexiglas. On each were scenes
from the story they'd just heard. Cooper was right.
With the lights on, the drama of the presentation
was gone, and the jumble of electrical cords and
duct tape made everything look homemade. On the
other hand, he was completely wrong.

"It doesn't ruin the magic," Jorie said as she
leaned down to examine the Harpers Ferry scene.
"It's a whole different kind of magic."

He pointed at a scout positioned behind a tree
on the road leading away from the ferry. "This guy
look familiar?"

She squinted. "Is that Hamburglar?"

Cooper started to laugh. "Sure is."

"Oh, no," Jorie said. "I thought they were all
those fussy miniatures you can buy. That's why the
army guys are in the donation box."

"Yep."

Now that she looked closer, she realized the entire diorama, all six or seven tables were made from junk. Toys? She wasn't sure what to call them. Someone—Marty, she supposed—had painstakingly painted each figure to disguise its origins and turn it into a Union or Confederate soldier, cavalry horse or civilian. She couldn't imagine the investment of time this must have taken.

They stayed longer in the room with the lights on than they had with the lights off, because every time Jorie thought she'd seen the last bit, she noticed one more detail. And Cooper had an infinite amount of information to share with her.

"How many times have you been here, exactly?" she asked.

"Too many to count. The first time I was a sophomore in high school. Hey, want to see what I contributed?"

He led her back to the scene at the beginning showing Lee poring over maps in his tent. "I drew the map. Pretty awesome, isn't it?"

She'd need a magnifying glass to confirm, but she knew even without checking that the map, done in Cooper's meticulous printing, was historically accurate and probably drawn to scale. On the way out, he flicked the lights off again.

"Marty doesn't like it when the atmosphere is spoiled."

"Marty should be proud of the work he did in there. I bet if he made turning the lights on part of the show, right at the end, he'd get more donations."

Cooper leaned past her to push open the door to the outside. She shivered again in the shade of the alley.

"Does Marty have a job?" she asked.

"He won't answer that question," Cooper said. "But I think he must."

"It's too bad he can't make a living with the museum. Imagine having that kind of crazy creative passion for something and being stuck working at something else." Jorie shook her head. "Money sucks, doesn't it?"

"Is the bakery that bad?"

"It's not the bakery. But I didn't give up my wedding planning business so I could box cupcakes and listen to Eliot tell jokes." She pulled him to a stop and put her arms around him so she could hide her face in his chest. "When is that stupid governor going to make up his mind, Cooper? Everything is on hold until he gives the okay for your appointment."

"We're not on hold," he said.

But they were. Under the surface of every minute they spent together was the knowledge that they were only together because of his brother. She did her level best to forget that, but she couldn't because they were living and breathing politics twenty-four hours a day.

If she didn't find some way to carve out her own life, she was going to lose her mind. The bakery really wasn't so bad, but she wasn't engaged by it. Alice did all of the real work—planning what to make for the week, ordering, baking, color schemes. She ran the tastings herself unless she was absolutely pushed, and then she let Jorie help.

The bakery was a great place for Alice, but for Jorie it was marking time. She needed something of her own, and soon.

JORIE WAS JUST GETTING out of the shower the next morning when Miriam called in a panic.

"Grace Blackwell is coming in this morning," she said. "She wants to donate three wishes, but she said they'll be of significant size so we'd better prepare press coverage."

"Sorry about that. I figured she might donate something if she was getting her picture taken. I bet Rachel knows someone who would come by and take pictures. We'll get them posted somewhere."

"Thanks, Jorie, but that's not why I called," Miriam said. "Or not entirely. Can you come in and volunteer for a few hours this morning?"

"Sure. What do you need?"

"Well, ever since we opened this registry idea up to the public, I've been inundated," Miriam said. "I guess I didn't realize how much work you and your mom did to get the registry filled. I need help."

"Sure. Let me know when."

"You can pick your hours. You'll be saving my life."

CHAPTER TWELVE

SHE AND MIRIAM laid out the two newest registries in the conference room and started to categorize the wishes. Chelsea had worked out a color-coding system and Jorie taught it to Miriam.

Jorie threw herself into the work, determined to get Miriam on a more secure footing before she left for the day. While they were discussing Grace's three wishes, they came up with a promotional campaign. They'd use Three Wishes to sell the idea that brides could choose their normal registry with a few wishes thrown in for good measure. Jorie sketched a design that looked like a cross between Aladdin's lamp and a high-heeled shoe. She and Miriam were convinced the brides would love it.

By the time three o'clock came, they'd made huge progress. Miriam perched on the edge of the conference room table with a mug of green tea. Jorie had a paper cup full of water. It was hardly a glamorous setting, but the offices were so familiar to her, she didn't notice the shabbiness anymore.

"Thank goodness we got so much done," Miriam

said. "I've been getting ready to post a job so I can hire someone permanent to help me, but I couldn't get far enough ahead to file the paperwork. Isn't that silly? I'm too busy to hire help."

Jorie's skin felt hot. Miriam was going to hire someone to work on her mom's Wish Registry? Someone would be here full-time doing the things she'd done today? Because she'd opened her own business directly after college, she'd never needed a résumé, but she was going to go home immediately and figure out how to write one. Cooper would know. He'd help her. She held her water cup so tightly it almost collapsed and she had to ease back on her grip. "It's not silly. The fact you need to hire someone is a great sign, isn't it?"

"You're exactly right," Miriam said.

Jorie took a sip of the water but couldn't even feel it going down. She couldn't believe she was this nervous, but it had been a while since she'd asked for something she really wanted. And she really wanted this. "Miriam, will you let me know when you post the job?"

"Do you want to be on the interview committee? We could use your insight."

"No. I'd like to apply."

Miriam was quiet just long enough to make Jorie thoroughly nervous. She shouldn't have said anything. She should have sent her résumé in like everybody else and then Miriam wouldn't be in the awkward position she was in right now—having to discourage her. They would need someone with financial experience. Someone who'd done fund-raising before. There must be a million qualifications for a job like this and she'd just exposed her own naïveté.

"Jorie, you wouldn't have to apply," Miriam said. "If you want the job, you're hired."

"What?"

"This is your idea. You and your mom put the program together. You know the structure from both sides. You'd be my ideal partner."

"Ideal?" Jorie's mind could barely keep up with the conversation.

"What about your business?"

"I closed it. I…weddings weren't fun anymore."

"Well, we'll have fun. Don't worry about that."

Jorie felt shocked. "Did I just apply for a job?"

"I just hired you, so I think you must have." Miriam pushed the box of tissues closer to her, but Jorie wasn't crying. She was ecstatic. "I do have to file paperwork so you won't be officially hired until we do that. There's a background check and I'll need references, but it's just formalities. Oh, Jorie, wouldn't your mom be thrilled?"

Jorie nodded. "She would be, I think. She really would be."

That was the truth, but Jorie wasn't taking this job for her mom. She was taking it for herself. She wanted to see what it was like to do work that made a lasting change in the world. She wanted to challenge herself to try things she'd never done, like fund-raising and scouting for donors. She wanted to work for herself, rather than be subjected to the whim of strangers. Most of all, Jorie was ready to start fresh.

SHE STOPPED BY THE bakery on her way home to let Alice know she'd need to put the Help Wanted sign back up.

"I'm thrilled for you!" Alice said. "And I won't mind looking for another counter helper. Eliot's sorted out now so I can try to hire someone to take the full-time hours and let him cut back again. It will work out great for everyone."

"I can stay as long as you need me," Jorie said.

"Thanks."

A text came in just then from Nolan. He wanted her to call him. She excused herself and stepped away from Alice toward the windows to give herself some privacy before she punched in his number.

"Jorie, there's a dinner tomorrow night at the Smith House and Cooper's going to need to be there. It's black-tie. We'll send a car for you at six. You'll be ready?"

It wasn't really a question and both of them knew it. "I'll be ready."

"I mentioned black-tie, right?"

"Yes, you did."

"Right. Six o'clock."

"Bye," she said, but he'd already hung up.

Alice had gone into the tasting room to set up for a family who were coming in for christening cake possibilities. "Can you believe they're bringing six children with them? I hope they like tiny pieces of cake."

"Remember Theresa Hogan? With the twelve bridesmaids and the gluten issue? They all came to the tasting."

"Right. And one of them brought her own container for leftovers."

"And then they didn't hire me anyway. Something Blue stole them away after the trunk show at The Gown Shoppe. You didn't even get the cake, did you?"

"Thank goodness. I wanted to poke a fork in my eye after the tasting. Sometimes it's better to turn a gig down before it ruins your life."

"Wiser words…" Jorie said. She picked up the stack of napkins and started rolling them to go into the silver rings. "Nolan just ordered me to make myself presentable for some dinner tomorrow at the Smith House. He mentioned it was black-tie twice, and not because he thought I didn't hear him. He just wanted to be sure I knew what that meant, I'm sure."

She put the first napkin down on the table and moved onto the next.

"You think he was always that overbearing or does it come from being in power for so long?"

"I don't know. Cooper's not like that. Thank God."

"So, the Smith House. That's probably the opera fundraiser. I wonder why they want you to go?"

"I have no idea, but it must be important. I wasn't given the option of begging off."

"You have a dress?"

"I do."

"Got some bling? Those opera ladies do it up. You're going to need to sparkle if you want to fit in."

Jorie finished the last napkin. "I have bling," she said.

JORIE WENT UP THE STAIRS and into her house without turning on the lights. Nolan's phone call had poisoned the triumphant feeling she'd had about her job. No matter what she did, she couldn't escape the feeling that this arrangement with Cooper was wrong. She didn't want to be trading perfect deportment for his ring on her finger.

In the living room, she switched on the lamp on the sideboard and retrieved the key for the drawer where she kept her mother's jewelry. The key was hidden in an envelope taped inside her copy of *Wuthering Heights*. When the drawer slid open, she ran her hand over the pieces. They were beautiful even if they represented failure. Every time one of her mom's guys rejected her, Jorie had felt the rejection, too. She grew up with the idea that the most important thing in the world was to be picked by a man.

Her mom had made sure that Jorie got picked. She'd found Cooper and then spent her last wish on a fairy-tale wedding. Of course, the ending wasn't turning out exactly the way fairy tales did. Her mom was gone, and even if Jorie did, by some miracle, wind up walking down the aisle, Chelsea wouldn't be with her. Cooper had broken up with her once, and now they'd gotten back together for business reasons.

She was being ordered around by Nolan—told where to go and how to dress. She might as well sort through these pieces her mom had given her and find the one that would suit her charade at the black-tie dinner.

COOPER HELD THE STACK of stapled pages up in front of his mouth to hide his yawn.

"Am I boring you, son?" Nolan asked.

"No," Cooper lied.

He and his dad were sitting in upholstered chairs on either side of the desk in Bailey's office. He supposed at some point he was going to have to get familiar with sitting in the big leather chair behind the desk, but not yet, thank goodness. He'd never been comfortable being the center of attention, so he'd put that ordeal off as long as he could.

He, Bailey and Nolan had spent the morning going over the legislation likely to come up for a vote while Cooper was the acting senator. He was familiar with some of it, but there were a few pieces he'd never seen before. The part he really needed help with was understanding the power structure surrounding each item. Bailey and his dad had given him a cheat sheet outlining the main players and their positions.

When they finished that, Bailey was dismissed and Cooper and his dad stayed to go over details of how he was supposed to vote in each case.

"You can't walk around this town blind," Nolan said. "When you were writing speeches it was okay if you didn't have the details on all of Bailey's work, but if you're going to be the point man now, you have to have all of this at your fingertips."

"I know."

"Good." Nolan pointed to a bill halfway down

the page. "Let's go through the school funding again."

Cooper hoped he wouldn't yawn again, but he was beyond bored and closing in on comatose. It wasn't that he found the subject tedious. He'd been working in politics for years and was highly successful at writing motivating, creative speeches about issues very similar to the ones Nolan was discussing.

The difference was the speechwriting was his work...his craft. The studying he was doing with his dad was more like cramming for a test than actually doing work. He needed to memorize predetermined votes and absorb his dad's point of view. He wasn't bringing anything to this process. He supposed it made sense that no one was asking his opinion, since he was supposed to be only a temporary appointee, but in the meantime, his relationship with his dad was starting to suffer. Every time he tried to add his own input to the discussion, Nolan reminded him that he was just a placeholder for his cousin.

Theo couldn't get elected soon enough.

THE FRONT OF THE HOUSE was dark when Cooper got there. He should have called, but he'd expected Jorie to be home. Or to tell him if she wasn't going to be there. He almost turned around and went to his own place, then decided to go in and wait. Maybe she'd run to the market or stopped for a drink with Alice and Eliot. After the day he'd spent pretending to be a senator, he really wanted to see Jorie and try to get his sanity back. He scanned the sidewalk in both directions and told himself he wasn't looking for creeps like the guy who attacked Jorie, but he didn't believe himself.

The street was empty, so he went up the steps and let himself in. When he flipped on the light in the living room, he saw that the top drawer was missing from the sideboard. That drawer was usually locked—he'd tried to open it once when he was looking for a corkscrew.

He didn't like the way this felt. Jorie should have been here. She should have cooked dinner or gotten takeout a couple hours ago and he should smell it, but the apartment was completely clean. There was no evidence she'd been there all day. So why was the drawer missing from the sideboard?

The guy he'd beaten up was still in jail—charges of resisting arrest and assaulting an officer would keep him there for a while—but that didn't mean some other snarling lowlife couldn't have forced his way into Jorie's home.

Where the hell was she?

He dropped his laptop bag on the couch and picked up the heavy marble bookend from the shelf near the window. He called out, "Jorie?"

She didn't answer.

"Jorie!"

When he poked his head around the corner, her bedroom door was closed and he didn't see a light underneath. His cell phone was in his pocket and he pulled it out, holding it in his left hand with his thumb over the emergency speed dial button while he hefted the bookend in his right.

"Jorie?" he called again, willing her to answer.

"In here."

He dropped the bookend, narrowly missing his toe, and let out a perfectly satisfying curse. She'd scared him half to death. What the hell was she doing?

Leaving the bookend on the floor, he pushed her door open. "Why didn't you answer me when I yelled for you? Why are all the lights off?"

He was all set to be righteously angry until he got a look at her, and then it was impossible to be mad because she had clearly lost her mind. "Are you playing pirates?"

She was sitting cross-legged in the middle of the bed, the drawer from the sideboard in front of her. She was wearing eight or nine necklaces, a ring on every finger, and had bracelets lined up her arms. Earrings were scattered in front of her. She looked exactly like a pirate queen counting her booty.

"It's my mom's jewelry," she said quietly. "Mine

now, I guess. She called it my inheritance. What was that noise? Did you drop something?"

"My weapon." She didn't respond. "I thought you'd been robbed. I wasn't sure if you were okay. I was going to bean the perp with your marble bookend."

He'd been ready to laugh, but she looked sad. Lost. He realized that whatever this was, it was serious to her. He sat gently on the edge of the bed.

She touched his wrist. "That was sweet, Cooper. Thank you."

"If I knew what you've been hiding in the drawer, I might have been even more worried. That's a lot of stuff, you know? Is it real?"

"Most of it. My mom got a lot of gifts over the years." She shoved a pile of papers toward him. "There's a stock account, too. She kept it for me."

"I don't know what to say. That's amazing."

"It makes me ashamed. I don't like to look at it." She started to take off the rings, lining them up on the felt in the bottom of the drawer one by one. "I was going to give it all away after she died. Just get rid of it, so I wouldn't have to think about her or how we lived. I couldn't, though, because she wanted me to have it. So I stuffed it in the drawer and hoped I could forget about it." She fumbled with the clasp of the diamond tennis bracelet she wore and he reached for her wrist. The clasp was

complicated, but he found the spring release and it
snapped open. He pulled the bracelet down over her
fingers and put it in the drawer. She turned away
from him and lifted her hair.

He undid the first necklace. Her skin was warm
to the touch and he brushed against her neck, watching the goose bumps form. He held the ends of the
necklace open, pulling it off. She didn't speak, just
waited, hair pulled up, neck bent, her posture trust-
ing and vulnerable.

He'd seen Chelsea in action. Of course, she'd
been sick almost the whole time he knew her, but
that hadn't stopped her from wrapping every single
therapist, intern and technician on her floor around
her little finger.

He'd never forget the chill he felt the night she
explained her wish to him. "I want you to take care
of Jorie," she'd whispered, her beautiful blue eyes
so serious, pulling him into an almost intimate
space. "Can you do that for me, Cooper? Give her
the wedding I never had and then take care of her
for me?"

His brother had asked him over and over to explain exactly how she convinced him, but he couldn't
explain it. Chelsea Burke had been a remarkable
woman with a talent for convincing people to do
exactly what she wanted.

Because he wasn't sure what was going on with

Jorie and she wasn't giving him any clues, he kept on as he'd started, silently removing each necklace, touching her carefully and only as part of the task. Each time their skin connected, he shuddered, the connection was so ripe with tension.

The last necklace was a long, twisted loop of pearls with a big jeweled flower at the end. It didn't have a clasp so he lifted it over her hair, letting his knuckles skim her cheeks, then put it into the drawer with the rest.

She let her hair fall down and lifted her eyes to meet his. He couldn't stand to see her looking defeated and defenseless.

"What's wrong, Jorie?"

"She did the best she could." She shook her head, her lips pressed together. "You know, anyone could criticize her and the Lord knows, I did. She used men and let them use her and she probably could have changed if she'd wanted to. Or if she'd been willing to settle for something less. But she was trying to make a life for me."

She looked at the jewels, each piece laid out carefully in the drawer. He had no idea what to say. No idea what she wanted.

"She was amazing. I only knew her for a little while, but I fell in love with her right along with everybody else."

"Your dad called today. We're supposed to go to a dinner tomorrow night."

Cooper nodded. "The opera thing at the Smith House, right?"

"I thought I'd find something in here to wear. But I can't do it."

"You don't have to."

"But I'm playing a part. The same way she always did. What makes me any different?"

"You're not her, Jorie. Before you agreed to all this, you made sure it wouldn't be a part. You demanded that. Remember? You said we had to start from scratch."

"I know, but—"

"But it's hard. I get that. Your mom taught you some screwed-up stuff and it's hard to get away from that. But you have to try if we're going to work."

"What are you saying? Should I sell these pieces? And do what with the money? It would always be tainted."

"So change that. Make it your own. Do the same thing you did with our wedding. Accept the gift your mom offered, but on your own terms."

Jorie stared at the drawer full of jewelry. What did Cooper mean? This jewelry was as much a part of her memories of her mom as her generous spirit, her deep love for a well-wrapped gift, her inability to carry a tune or her need to keep searching for someone to love her.

She ran her hand over the rings, watching the light play on the faceted jewels. They winked like fairy lights on the dark velvet drawer liner.

Like wishes...

"I was waiting to see you in person to tell you I got a job today."

"Seriously?" He grinned at her. "I didn't even know you were applying."

"I didn't either. I'm going to work for Miriam. She needs a colleague to help with the bridal registry."

"Jorie, that's perfect for you. I'm thrilled."

"So, that got me thinking." She picked up a set of sapphire earrings. "What if these earrings turned into summer camp for a foster child?"

"What?"

"You said to transform them. What if we turned them into wishes?"

He picked up the rope of pearls. "This looks exactly like a wheelchair ramp."

She scooped two garnet rings and the diamond tennis bracelet into a pile. "Disney World for a family of four. Or maybe six."

A stick pin, two bracelets and the sapphire pendant necklace converted a first-floor bathroom into a handicap accessible spa room.

They kept going until each item in the drawer had been dreamed into a new form.

Ever since Nolan's call that afternoon, she'd felt weighted down, but now she felt free. "Make love to me, Cooper? Please?"

HE KNELT BY THE EDGE of the bed. Jorie was amazing and she really had no clue. She'd gotten herself a perfect job and freed herself of an oppressive legacy, all the while keeping her integrity and protecting the memories of her mom. She was turning her life around and he was stuck in limbo. Waiting to do what his father and the governor told him, just as soon as they made up their minds.

He tilted her hips, scooting her to the edge of the bed so he could strip off her pants and underwear. Then, starting at the bottom, he unbuttoned her shirt, taking his time until it was hanging free from her shoulders and he could push it back and down her arms. He quickly took off his own clothes, then spread her legs so he could move between them. Reaching around her, he unhooked her bra and carefully took that off, too. When they were both naked, he sat back on his heels and looked at her.

"You're gorgeous," he said. He spread his hands

on her hips to pull her against him. "You amaze me, Jorie."

And then he took his time showing her exactly how he felt.

CHAPTER THIRTEEN

AROUND THE END of the fourth week, his dad decided they were going to start campaign strategy meetings without the governor's appointment. Karloski only had a few more days by law and they hadn't heard anything substantive to indicate he was thinking of someone besides Cooper.

Nolan gathered the family and a small team of staff at his house and they worked from breakfast straight through to the early evening. Two of the staff members left early—one quit and one was fired, but Cooper was pretty sure the firing was only temporary. Nolan had a quick temper and it was best to get out of his way when he aimed it at you, but he respected good work. He often fired people who were then seen back at their desks later the same day.

He finally agreed that they could break for dinner at seven. Cooper begged to be the one who went to get the pizzas because he thought he was going to go nuts if he didn't get out of the house for a few minutes.

On his way over to the pizza place, he called Jorie. She was finishing up with Miriam and said she'd be at his parents' house in twenty minutes.

He parked, and was on his way back with the pizzas when Bailey called him—Theo had switched all of his ringtones a few days ago so that it sounded like his pocket was barking. Since he was juggling three boxes and a plastic bag full of drinks he didn't answer. The call went to voice mail and then Bailey called right back. More barking.

He was going to kill Theo.

Jorie was coming toward him from the other direction and she jogged up, grabbing the pizza boxes so he could pull out his phone.

"Bailey, hey—" he started, but then he realized his brother was as close to crying as he'd ever heard him.

"Wait, what? Bay. Slow down."

Jorie looked at him, her eyes concerned, but they kept walking toward the house.

"Deb got hit by a car. It wasn't serious. I mean, it was. She felt fine. She even stood up, but they took her to the hospital anyway, because of the baby." Bailey's voice was shaking. "They put her on a monitor and, God, Coop. The baby. They think there's something wrong. They took her in for an emergency C-section."

"Okay." Cooper's thoughts were racing as fast as his heart. "What hospital? Where are you?"

"Mercy Heights."

"We'll be right there, Bay. Hang tight."

"Okay. All right."

Cooper was about to say goodbye when Bailey said, "Can you tell Mom? If I call she won't answer."

"Yeah. Sure. I'll tell her."

He clicked off his phone and met Jorie's eyes. "Deb's in the hospital. They're doing an emergency C-section. Sounds like the baby's having problems."

"Oh, Cooper. We have to go."

He unlocked the door and they went straight back to the kitchen, where his parents and Theo along with a few staff were waiting. His mom had her back to him when he blurted out the news. She turned, one hand covering her mouth, and shook her head quickly as if to deny what he'd just said.

"Where are they?" Nolan asked.

"Mercy Heights."

"Is he going to call and tell us what happens?"

Rachel looked quickly at his dad even as he felt Jorie step closer to his side.

"I told him I'd be there, Dad. He's on his own."

"Deb's family will go. They're probably on their way."

"Dad!"

Theo had backed up against the table and the staff huddled near him, looking anxiously at Nolan.

"Look, Cooper. There's nothing you or I or anyone can do there. The press is going to be all over the hospital and you know it. You don't want to make that circus worse."

"That circus is about Bailey's baby. He needs us to be there with him."

"Cooper's right," Jorie said. "I'm going with him."

"No one's going anywhere," Nolan shouted. "Bailey will call and let us know what happens. What help do you think you can give him? You're no doctor."

Cooper looked at his mom. What did she want him to do? He wanted to tell his father to go to hell. But would that be the final fracture that damaged his family for good?

JORIE WANTED TO SCREAM at Nolan the same way he was yelling at the rest of them. How dare he? How dare he reduce this moment to a press conference. How dare he try to make Cooper feel wrong for doing the right thing. How dare he make this an "us" v. "them" choice. Cooper was wavering and she didn't want to see him back down. He knew that going to the hospital was the right thing because he'd immediately promised Bailey he would. Maybe all he needed was someone to stand with him.

She dropped the pizza she was holding on the counter and they all looked at her. "We're going. Cooper and I will be at the hospital to support Bailey. We'll call as soon as there is news."

She hoped she hadn't just cut herself off. What if Cooper wasn't with her.

But then his hand took hers. She squeezed his fingers and felt an answering pressure.

"Cooper, be reasonable," Nolan said. "Your duty is to the family. Until Karloski—"

"Stop it," Rachel said. "Please stop it."

Nolan turned his angry eyes on her. She shook her head. "Enough is enough. Our grandchild is in the hospital, Nolan. We need to be there. That's where our family is."

"You're not thinking straight, Rachel."

"I know what I'm doing," she said quietly. "I've always known. This is what's right now."

"But the press—"

"Doesn't scare me."

Jorie thought she caught some undercurrents, as if Rachel and Nolan were having a shadow conversation only they could understand. On the surface, though, Rachel got her way.

"I have to be with him," she said simply. "Bailey is all that matters right now."

Nolan knocked the pizza onto the floor. "No. Nobody's going anywhere."

Jorie had never admired Rachel more than when she stepped carefully over and around the scattered pizzas to leave the kitchen. Nolan glared after her. "This is pointless," he called. "By the time you get there, it will all be over."

It didn't matter, Jorie thought, as she followed Rachel and Cooper down the long straight hall. Rachel's purse was on the back of the hall closet door. Cooper patted his pocket and found his keys.

"Everybody set?" he asked.

No one followed them when they left the house. Rachel looked toward the kitchen, but she didn't turn back.

When they got to the sidewalk, Cooper said he'd get his car and bring it around. He loped off and left Jorie and Rachel standing together.

Jorie wasn't sure what to say. Then she thought about her own mom and how Chelsea would know exactly what to do right now. She put an arm around Rachel's waist. "We'll be there before you know it," she said. "Bailey will be so glad you came."

Rachel put her hand over Jorie's. They stood together without talking until Cooper pulled his Jeep up out front. Jorie opened the back door and Rachel got in and then she motioned for the older woman to move over. "I'm going to sit back here with you," she said. "No sense worrying by yourself."

As soon as she closed the door, Cooper set off. He was focused on the road and the silence in the car was thick. Jorie guessed no one wanted to talk about what had just happened or to speculate on what they might be facing.

But then Rachel spoke.

"Nolan had an affair." Her hands were folded in her lap and her eyes were closed. "You boys were little. She was a regional coordinator in his campaign office and they were traveling together. I was busy at home and I wasn't paying attention."

"Mom?" Cooper's eyes were anxious in the rearview mirror.

"Shush. I need to say this. The woman called me. That was how I found out. He was furious with her, of course, and denied that it meant anything. I couldn't even look at him, I felt that betrayed. We left. You probably don't remember that, Cooper, do you? You and Bailey and I spent two weeks with my parents."

"I remember being at their house, but I didn't know why," Cooper said quietly.

"Well, in the end, I went back. I made the decision to go back to him and he swore he wouldn't do it again." Rachel glanced at Jorie. "It took a long time to trust him again. A lot of hard work, too. Cooper was almost in kindergarten so I started working with Nolan. I thought if I could connect our family to his job, it would help keep him close."

Cooper turned into the driveway of the hospital.

"That's why he couldn't run for Senate again after he lost the vice presidency. Someone uncovered evidence and they sent it to us. If your dad ran, they were going to put the story out."

"Mom, you never told us any of this. Not even when Bailey ran the first time."

"I know. I was...ashamed, I think. I didn't think it mattered. Your dad changed, you know. After we started working together, he didn't look around anymore."

"So when Bailey cheated..." Jorie said.

"I was furious with him. It brought back all of those feelings. Made me think about it when I've been so successful at not thinking about it. I let my anger get the best of me."

Cooper pulled over at the visitor's entrance and put on the flashers. "Mom, I don't know what to say."

"We don't have time to say anything now, but we can talk later. Once the baby is safe."

She and Jorie got out while Cooper went to park the Jeep. As they walked up the ramp to the hospital, Rachel touched her shoulder. "I've never stood up to

Nolan. Not on something like this. I think I've been afraid that if I rocked the boat, he'd leave me."

Jorie nodded. She knew how that felt. She'd watched her own mother struggle with similar issues more than once. Of course, when push came to shove, Chelsea had almost always chosen to stick to her guns, which meant she ended up alone. That was an interesting thought, and one she wanted to examine more closely, but Rachel was still talking.

"When you stood up for Cooper, backed him up in front of Nolan, I knew I couldn't stay behind. I've been in the habit of thinking of myself as part of Nolan's team. Maybe I need to start thinking of myself as an individual sometimes."

Jorie didn't know what to say. "I never would have guessed, Rachel. You are a…formidable woman. At least from the outside. Maybe you need to feel that more for yourself?"

"Maybe I do," she said.

A camera crew was outside the lobby doors and Rachel straightened her spine when she saw them. "Hold on tight, Jorie. We're going through this crowd together. This is something I know how to do."

The reporters called Rachel's name and threw what seemed like hundreds of questions at her in the time it took to go a few hundred feet from the doors to the elevators. Rachel kept one strong hand clamped on Jorie's wrist and steered her through the crowd, using the shoulders she'd earned from hours of tennis when she had to.

Soon enough, they were out of the crush and on the elevator. Rachel dropped Jorie's wrist and quietly used her fingers to wipe a few tears from her eyes.

"I will never forgive myself if something's wrong," she said. It wasn't a threat or an emotional outburst, more a statement of fact, and Jorie believed her.

"You're here now, Rachel. That matters."

"Yes, it does," she answered quietly.

THE BABY WAS A GIRL.

Cooper had been there about ten minutes when the doctor told Bailey that Deb was out of surgery and his little girl was holding her own. She was going to be in the neonatal intensive care unit until her lungs developed a bit more, but they had every reason to believe she'd be fine. His brother sank down into a chair. "Oh, thank God," he said quietly.

His mom sat in the chair next to Bailey, her arm across his shoulders. Bailey had been too scared earlier to remember he was angry with her, and now it looked as if their rift was on its way to being healed.

He searched for Jorie. She was standing in the

doorway on the other side of the room, watching his mom and brother. He crossed to her.

"We owe you," he whispered. "Thanks for getting us here."

"You knew you were supposed to be here," she said. "Your mom did, too."

"But you were the one who stood up to my dad." Cooper put his hands on her shoulders. "He's probably going to be pissed about that."

Jorie was still watching his mom and Bailey. "I don't know, Cooper. Your mom is pretty mad, too. If I were your dad, I'd be worrying about her a lot more than me."

"You'll tell me if he says anything, though, right?"

"Of course."

The nurse said Bailey could see his daughter and the whole group of them—Cooper, Rachel, Jorie, Deb's parents and younger sister—all trooped down to the viewing area outside the neonatal intensive care unit. The nurses showed Bailey the procedures for getting gowned properly and then took him inside. When he held his baby girl, even with all the needles and tubes trailing from her, she looked beautiful. Cooper put one arm around his sobbing mother and one arm around his dry-eyed fiancée and watched his brother and his niece. It had been a long time since there'd been a new Murphy. This one was having a tough start, but he was going to do everything he could to make sure she had an excellent life.

After about an hour, Deb was wheeled into the viewing area by a nurse. She looked exhausted and she had a large goose egg on her forehead, but as soon as she caught sight of Bailey and the baby, she started to cry.

Rachel had met Deb's parents and sister, and while they were slightly cool to her, no one had been rude. Now Cooper leaned down to ask if his mother wanted to meet Deb.

"Will you see if she minds, Coop? I don't want to upset the poor thing."

He approached Deb's wheelchair and waited until she was finished talking to her mom. "Congratulations," he said. "She's beautiful."

"Thank you," Deb said. "And thanks for coming."

"My mom is here, too. Would you mind if she says hi?"

Deb looked uncertain. She glanced toward Bailey, but he was occupied with the baby. "Okay," she said finally.

He reached for his mom's hand and drew her forward. "Deb, meet my mom, Rachel."

Both women had tears in their eyes when they embraced.

"I'm so terribly sorry that I've waited this long

to get to know you," Rachel said. "I hope you'll forgive me, even though my behavior has been inexcusable."

It would have taken a much harder heart than Deb's not to accept such a sincere apology. By the time they left the hospital, Cooper was sure the two women were on their way to a warm relationship. He had dibs on teaching the kid how to drive, but it was clear he was going to have to line up behind his mom to get at her any other time.

LATER, AFTER THEY DROPPED Rachel at home and went to a late-night drive-through for burgers, they were lying in Jorie's bed.

"I realized something about my mom tonight," she said.

"Me, too." He stroked her shoulder. "You first."

"All this time, I thought she gave everything up for her men. I saw her chasing that ring and hoping for vows and I believed she failed."

"But?"

"But she had principles. She got dumped too many times. Obviously. People get dumped. But sometimes she dumped the men. She took me and left because whatever the guy had to offer her wasn't good enough."

He smiled into her hair.

"Your mom was a force of nature. I've been saying that all along."

"Well, I guess it took talking to your mom and hearing how much she gave up to keep your dad to make me realize all the times my mom made the opposite choice."

"I can't believe my dad cheated. I have to ask Bay if he remembers anything about it, but I don't think he does. He would have told me."

"It's been quite a night."

"How about that baby," he said. "She looked smart, didn't she?"

He felt her smile. "She sure did, Coop. Takes after her uncle, I'm sure."

"I hope she doesn't get quite as tall as me."

"She'll be perfect. You know that." She slid her leg in between his. "Are you tired?"

"Not much," he lied.

It turned out she wasn't very tired either.

EVENTUALLY, SHE FELL asleep with her head on his chest. He lifted her carefully to the side so he could grab his notebook. The page where he'd started his vows so long ago was getting cluttered. He found an empty spot and wrote, "I promise never to cheat." And then "I promise to pay attention." And finally, "If you call me, I'll always come."

He was ready.

If he'd broken up with her because he couldn't write his vows, he now knew he was ready to ask her to marry him again.

She wanted to wait until after Theo was sworn in and he understood her reasoning, but on the other hand, he was impatient. This charade of an engagement caused her problems. He could see that.

He went back to bed eventually, but he didn't sleep much. He wished he knew the right thing to do.

NOLAN SENT A TEXT that Cooper should take the day off. He suspected his mom was behind it, but he didn't risk calling to find out. He and Jorie packed a bag full of water bottles, her digital camera, and sunscreen, and escaped to the Mall. They wandered all morning, looking at the monuments, buying hot dogs from a cart, browsing in her favorite bookstore, tucked in an alley and full of wonderful stuff. They argued over which year the Lincoln Memorial was finished, who had a better cavalry, the Confederacy or the Rohirrim from *The Lord of the Rings,* and generally enjoyed the hell out of each other.

Bailey called and told him they'd named the baby Mary Anne. Mary was Deb's mom's middle name and Anne was Rachel's. They were planning to call her Mamie. That led them into a conversation about nicknames.

"Everyone always asks if my real name is Jordan," Jorie said. "But I'm plain Jorie. When I was little, my mom used to call me JB, which I thought stood for Jorie Burke, but she swore stood for Just Bratty."

"Nobody better call Mamie a brat. They'll have to answer to her uncle."

"Did you have a nickname when you were a kid?"

"Bailey called me dorkweasel for about three months when I was in first grade until my dad made him write an essay on the habitat and breeding habits of the weasel. Does dorkweasel count?"

He waited patiently while she stopped laughing and then he kissed her. A group of high school students passing by whistled and snickered. He kissed her some more. One of the teenagers snapped a picture with his phone. Cooper rested his forehead on hers. "That's it, Jorie. I'm keeping you."

"I'm so happy about that," she said. Her eyes sparkled. "Dorkweasel."

"I shouldn't have told you that, should I?"

"Probably not."

His phone rang and he reached in his pocket to pull it out, still looking at Jorie. He liked the way the sun made her eyes a bright blue. The caller ID told him it was his dad. He wondered what the chances were he could get away with saying he'd lost his phone. But he knew Nolan would just try Jorie if he didn't pick up.

He answered, but kept his arm around Jorie. "Dad, you told me I could have the day off, remember? One whole day?"

"The governor made his decision," his dad said. "It's good news."

CHAPTER FOURTEEN

"THANK GOD," Cooper said. "Wow. Great. Took him long enough." He wasn't making any sense, but he was overwhelmed. He was going to be a temporary senator after all. It was a lot to take in.

"Well, there's a condition. The seat is yours, but remember when I told you they had questions? Well, the questions weren't about you, they were about Theo. The state committee doesn't want to swap one Murphy for another a second time in one year. They think it looks bad. Theo's age is working against him. And that video of you and the mugger really made an impression. They think they can get a lot of campaign mileage out of it."

"Dad, what the hell are you talking about?"

"They want you, Cooper. As the appointee and the candidate. Theo's off the table."

"I never agreed to that, Dad."

"Cooper!" His dad's voice exploded through the line. "Don't even think about starting with me. We got this far, we'll work out the rest of it. The state committee wants you. You've got the connections.

Your mom and I can make sure the transition team is in place so when you take over for Bailey we'll keep the issues to a minimum. It makes sense you're nervous, but we'll all be right there with you, same team as always."

Cooper shook his head. He wasn't worried about being a freaking United States Senator.

He'd been thinking about Jorie. This day had given him a taste of what it would be like once they were both free from the staged engagement and his family's business. He wanted to marry Jorie, but on her terms, not his. And not under the cloud of his election. He'd been waiting to talk to her, looking forward to the day when he was sure she was ready for him to propose again, this time for real. Taking the Senate seat would make that impossible.

"What if I said no? What's the Plan B?"

"There isn't a Plan B, Cooper. If someone tells you they want you to run for the Senate, you god damn well better say yes because they're not going to ask again."

That was the problem. His dad hadn't expected to be out of the Senate so young. As long as he had a son holding a seat, he could stay involved, broker deals, draft legislation. The prestige wasn't the same, but there was little difference in the power level.

If he said no and Theo had already been rejected,

there wouldn't be a Murphy in the Senate. His mom and dad would have to retire for real, long before they'd planned to.

Any refusal on his part would tear his family apart again. The faults they'd exposed after Bailey quit, and then again last night scared him. He'd always thought the Murphys were unbreakable, but now he saw the cracks. How could he stand to be the one who ripped apart the bonds they'd repaired last night?

"I have to talk to Jorie," he said. "I'll call you in a little bit."

"Son, make sure she understands that this changes everything. You're going to have to work things out with her to make it through the election and at least a year. We can set her up with a house—"

"Dad. Stop talking. I'm hanging up."

He turned off his phone. He didn't know when she'd shifted out from under his arm, but she was standing a few feet away on the path now. She knew. He could tell how stiff she was—the opposite of the person he'd just been kissing.

"Did you hear him yelling or did you guess?"

"Both." She smiled. "Congratulations."

"The state committee wants me to run. I don't see how I can say no."

Did she shiver? He couldn't tell. He stepped closer to her. "Should we go home so we can talk?"

"Is there anything to talk about? You want to run,

don't you? You've always been the support guy and this is your chance to take center stage. Why would you refuse?"

He clenched his fists. "I never wanted the seat. I know it seems odd, but I like being the support guy. I'm a speechwriter and I'm good at it. But maybe I could want it. Maybe I need to give it a chance. Find the things in it that are going to work for me. I wasn't expecting this, but maybe it could be good for us."

She came to him and slid her arms around his waist, grabbing his belt in the back. He felt better. Maybe what he'd said was true. This might be the start of something wonderful for both of them.

"I'm with you, Cooper. You know that."

JORIE RODE WITH COOPER to Bailey's office but didn't go in. He apologized for having to end their day early, but she reassured him it was okay. The last thing he needed was to worry about her. She walked home alone slowly.

She could head over to the Wish Team and work for a while. She and Miriam had a bunch of really great projects on the go. She could call Alice. Her friend would be at her door in ten minutes. She'd even bring cake. She could also call Rachel if she wanted to.

Life was different for her than it had been when Cooper broke up with her the first time. She'd changed, she'd opened up, she'd discovered that she could count on people.

She even had her fiancé back for good. He wouldn't break up with her again. Not with the election coming up. She knew he wanted to marry her. She wanted to marry him, too. Everything should be perfect. It was perfect. The trouble was inside her, as usual.

She was going to marry Cooper. She loved him. He loved her. There was absolutely no reason not to marry him. Except they'd never had a chance to choose. She'd thought they had time. After the appointment and the election, after Theo was sworn in, she'd expected to have time to herself with Cooper. They weren't getting that now. They were getting something even better, in his dad's mind. A Senate seat. A guarantee that the Murphy legacy would continue.

She shouldn't care about the choosing part. Cooper would have picked her. She knew it. She just wished he'd had the chance, because there was always going to be a little piece inside Chelsea Burke's daughter waiting to get rejected. She just hoped it was small enough not to poison the rest of what they had.

COOPER GOT BACK late that night. Jorie realized she'd been expecting him even though he hadn't said he'd be coming. He would want to see her, though. Of course he would.

She'd worn the blue nightgown on purpose. If they had sex, she could stop thinking. And she didn't want to talk.

When he came through the bedroom door, she had a candle lit on the nightstand. His eyes took a few seconds to adjust, but then he saw her.

"We should talk," he said.

"Please, Cooper. We can talk tomorrow."

He nodded once and then undressed and came to her.

She held his face in her hands and kissed him long and hard, her tongue seeking as he ran his hands over her back, shoulders, breasts, hips, thighs. He wasn't shy about his need, letting her see and feel how much he wanted her. She wished she felt the same way he did, but there was something in the way. She believed that he loved her. She trusted him. It was just the small voice in the back of her head telling her she'd never know now. She'd never be sure.

She'd gotten as much time as she was ever going to get to prove to him and to herself that they were going to make it. In the end, they'd run out of time. They'd gotten back together in a sham engagement and they'd work together now to make it real. Those were facts and nothing would change them. It had to be enough.

She lay back, pulling him with her, and then rolled him over so she could climb on top of him, fitting their bodies together, feeling him touching every part of her. There were condoms in the nightstand and she handed one to him. When he was inside her, she shut her eyes, doing everything she could to turn off her brain so she could let this man, this beautiful, smart, kind and loyal man love her.

Afterward, she lay in his arms and listened to him sleep. The sweat was drying on their skin, leaving a thin shivery cold sheen, but she couldn't find the energy to pull the sheet up. She wondered if there was a way they could stay here, just like this, forever. She thought she'd be okay then. Here in the dark, with his arms around her, she could believe.

That wouldn't happen, though. His family was waiting for him and tomorrow reality would come bearing down on them. She started to feel the old panic and slipped out of bed. She didn't want to disturb him when he was going to be so busy in the next few months.

COOPER FELT HER GO. He'd been asleep, but ever since the night that guy attacked her, he'd had trouble sleeping if she wasn't nearby. Something was wrong. She was putting up a good front but she wasn't happy.

He wasn't happy either. The meetings he'd had were terrible. He kept waiting for someone to jump up and point at him and say, "Fraud," because he sure as hell didn't feel like a senator.

His mom had kept an eye on him. Every once in a while, he'd notice her staring, but she hadn't told him what was bothering her. Maybe she knew he was the wrong choice. Maybe she could persuade his dad.

He lay awake for a while, hoping Jorie would come back to bed. When she finally did, he closed his eyes and pretended he'd been asleep all along.

CHAPTER FIFTEEN

HIS DAD WAS INSANE. Cooper suspected he'd stayed up all night and now he was back at it, driving them crazy at the crack of dawn.

The first text had come at what felt like five minutes after he fell asleep. He didn't answer that one, so his dad called. Then he texted again.

Cooper finally gave in and got up to take a shower. He left his phone outside the bathroom, and when he came out, there were fourteen new texts and two voice mails.

"Is there any chance that your dad is actually a preteen girl?" Jorie asked. She was sitting at her small kitchen table with a cup of coffee, one strap of her blue nightgown sliding down her shoulder. "He texts more than anyone I know."

"He's excited."

"He should be. This is a big day for the Murphys, right?"

Cooper slid his belt through the loops and cinched it. "Big day. That's right."

"What's the game plan?"

Another text hit his screen and he missed what she said.

"What?"

"I asked what's the game plan?"

I give up my life and any hope of an honest relationship with the woman I love so my dad can keep walking the floors of the Senate. "Uh, what?"

"Are you supposed to be somewhere this morning?"

I'm supposed to be in my dad's library listening to him tell me what to do and how to do it. I'll be there every morning for the rest of my life. "I'm not..."

Jorie got up. "Are you okay?"

Other than feeling that he was going to vomit? Yep. He was perfectly fine.

"No." He felt behind him for the edge of the couch and then sat down. "No. I'm not okay."

She sat next to him, the hem of her nightgown riding up. He put one hand on her thigh, touching that special soft spot just to reassure himself that he wasn't losing his mind. He was sitting on the couch with Jorie and he wasn't going to tell his dad he couldn't accept the nomination.

Except, he really thought he had to.

"What's the matter?"

"I didn't know what was the matter. Not until just now, but I think I figured it out."

She waited. He waited.

"Yes?" she prompted. "You figured it out?"

"I'm the only one who's not a cheater. Bailey can't be the senator because he's a cheater, or maybe he's a cheater because he didn't want to be the senator. Either way the result is the same. And my dad can't be the senator because he's a cheater. So we need a senator and guess what?"

She shook her head.

"The only Murphy who never, ever, wanted to be the senator has to be the senator because he's the only one who found the right person to marry and he's the only one who will never cheat. Ever." He touched that soft spot again. "I mean me. I would never cheat. But that doesn't mean I'd be a good senator."

Her eyes were glistening. Why was she crying?

"Why are you crying?"

"I'm not crying. I'm listening."

"We both got caught, right? Your mom wanted you to get married and she gave you her wish. You didn't get to choose. And my dad wants that seat and he's only got one way to get it. I don't get to choose." Cooper turned to face her. "I'm going to tell him no. All along I kept telling myself I had to take care of my family. Which is the right answer, but I had the wrong family in mind. I have to take care of you and me."

"Cooper. You can't tell him no."

"Yes. I can. I can absolutely tell him no. I should tell him no because I really, really don't want to be a senator. And you can tell me no. Your mom shouldn't have put this on you. How could you say no to her last wish? I never should have gone along with it. It seemed romantic, but it was just as manipulative as the stuff my dad pulls."

JORIE COULD FEEL THE tears on her face, but she still didn't quite believe she was crying. She hadn't cried in months. Why now? Because Cooper said he would never cheat? That he'd found the right person to marry? But then why was he telling her she could say no to him?

"Are you breaking up with me again?" she asked.

"Yes."

One simple word and it landed like a rock in her gut. He was jumping all over the place.

"Why?"

"So you can choose. Free and clear. When you're ready." He took his notebook out of his pocket and tapped it on his knee. "I've got notes in here, Jorie. All the things I'm going to vow. I'll propose again as soon as you're ready. But this time it's your choice. Nobody else's."

"I still don't understand," she said.

"I love you, Jorie. I want to spend my life with

you. But we need to start the right way. With our own lives and our own goals and our own dreams."

"Are you really not going to be the senator?"

"I can't. I hate public speaking. I hate committees. I'm not a huge fan of politicians, and without Bailey around, I found out I really, really, don't like working for my dad."

"What will your parents do?"

"They're going to live their own lives. Same as Bailey. And me. And you."

"What are you going to do?"

Cooper smiled and leaned back on the couch. He lifted her up to hold her on his lap, one hand resting warm and strong on her hip, the other holding her hand. "I might apply at the Wish Team. I write a mean fundraising letter and I have experience with fulfilling wishes."

This was not the conversation she'd expected to have when she was pouring her coffee and listening to his phone go crazy with texts and calls. But that was Cooper Murphy to a T. He didn't do what she expected. He led with his heart and when he did… he was unstoppable.

"I'm not sure we have any positions open," Jorie said. "Is your résumé very impressive?"

His hand crept up under the hem of her gown and cupped her bottom. "I have skills, Jorie. Skills you haven't even dreamed of."

"We have a rigorous interview procedure," she said, dipping her head to kiss his lips and then to nip his earlobe. "And if you did get hired, there would be performance reviews."

"Annually?" Cooper asked. His hand was working its way around the side of her hip and she found herself turning, opening herself to meet him.

"Daily."

"Hot dog," Cooper said. "I think I've found the job for me."

She spun around to straddle him and captured his hands under her knees. She applied gentle pressure to keep them pinned. She didn't want to be distracted when she asked him her next question and Cooper's hands were very distracting.

"What if I don't want to be engaged right now?"

He closed his eyes but opened them again quickly. "That's all right. It's what I've been telling you."

"I...I think I might not want to be engaged."

"That's okay. I can wait."

He kept his voice steady and she gave him enormous credit for that. He couldn't conceal the hurt in his eyes, though.

"I'm really sick of being engaged. And I really don't want to plan a wedding right now."

"That's all okay. We'll keep on the way we've been, but skip the engagement."

"Or we could just go to a justice of the peace and get it over with."

He bit his bottom lip then burst out laughing. "That's your proposal? I made you a freaking book, Jorie. I drew things and wrote little funny stories and you say 'let's get it over with?'"

"You want to do it?"

"Let me have my hands back," he said. She lifted her knees and he put his hands on her shoulders, drawing her toward him so he could feather kisses on her eyelids, her forehead, her cheeks, her mouth.

"You could ask me if I'm up for a trip to the moon, and I'd say yes. I'm in, Jorie. Wherever you go, I'm in."

"Well, I'll just go get dressed. Looks like I'm going to be a June bride, after all."

She slipped off his lap and ran for the bedroom, but stuck her head back out and said, "We are not skipping the cake. Red velvet from Lucky's. My treat."

EPILOGUE

BEFORE THEY GOT MARRIED, of course, they had to tell his dad that he wasn't going to be able to accept that Senate job after all.

He thought his dad was going to kill him with his bare hands. Nolan's face turned red and he tipped a table over. Cooper actually stepped in front of Jorie to protect her, which was something he thought only B actors did in old Westerns. But when his dad paused in his tirade to suck in a breath so he could yell some more, he heard his mom say, "Excuse me. I have a proposition to make."

The look on Nolan's face was priceless when Rachel said she'd recently decided that she wouldn't mind running for office and if none of her boys were going to be the senator, she'd like to throw her hat in the ring. Pride. Love. Delight. The eager anticipation of many more years of strategizing and power brokering hand in hand with the woman he loved. Well, Cooper didn't think there was a word for the exact expression on his dad's face, but whatever it was, he was glad he'd been there to see it.

Jorie cried again. It was becoming a regular habit with her, but he didn't mind a bit.

Governor Karloski was furious to see his power play dissolve as the Murphys got their way once again, but he couldn't stop Rachel's candidacy. Couldn't even hint that he'd like to stop it. The first lady of Pennsylvania politics was not only smart, powerful, articulate and well connected, she was *beloved*. One strategically placed news story describing Rachel's disappointment at being denied the nomination would not only have killed Karloski's reelection chances, it would have sparked a full-on voter revolt. Maybe even a write-in campaign.

Not every detail Cooper had imagined in his fairy tale came true, of course. There was no wedding with tulle and top hats, just a quiet ceremony in front of a justice of the peace. Jorie did meet his college friends at a reunion and they did call him Lefty, but he never did make her shrimp kebabs even though he continued to like food on sticks.

The day Rachel Murphy was sworn in as the senator from Pennsylvania, she had a party. Jorie came out of retirement to plan it for her and every detail was perfect. Around midnight, after the last slice of cake was eaten but the band was still going strong, Jorie led Cooper onto the dance floor. He did his best with the fox trot and she smiled as he stepped on her toes while she hummed "Love and Marriage" along with the band.

* * * * *

COMING NEXT MONTH

Available July 12, 2011

HSRCNM0611

REQUEST YOUR FREE BOOKS!
2 FREE NOVELS PLUS 2 FREE GIFTS!

Harlequin

Super Romance

Exciting, emotional, unexpected!

USA TODAY *bestselling author B.J. Daniels takes you on a trip to Whitehorse, Montana, and the Chisholm Cattle Company.*

RUSTLED

Available July 2011 from Harlequin Intrigue.

As the dust settled, Dawson got his first good look at the rustler. A pair of big Montana sky-blue eyes glared up at him from a face framed by blond curls.

A woman rustler?

"You have to let me go," she hollered as the roar of the stampeding cattle died off in the distance.

"So you can finish stealing my cattle? I don't think so." Dawson jerked the woman to her feet.

She reached for the gun strapped to her hip hidden under her long barn jacket.

He grabbed the weapon before she could, his eyes narrowing as he assessed her. "How many others are there?" he demanded, grabbing a fistful of her jacket. "I think you'd better start talking before I tear into you."

She tried to fight him off, but he was on to her tricks and pinned her to the ground. He was suddenly aware of the soft curves beneath the jean jacket she wore under her coat.

"You have to listen to me." She ground out the words from between her gritted teeth. "You have to let me go. If you don't they will come back for me and they will kill you. There are too many of them for you to fight off alone. You won't stand a chance and I don't want your blood on my hands."

"I'm touched by your concern for me. Especially after you just tried to pull a gun on me."

"I wasn't going to shoot you."

Dawson hauled her to her feet and walked her the rest of the way to his horse. Reaching into his saddlebag, he pulled out a length of rope.

"You can't tie me up."

He pulled her hands behind her back and began to tie her wrists together.

"If you let me go, I can keep them from coming back," she said. "You have my word." She let out an unladylike curse. "I'm just trying to save your sorry neck."

"And I'm just going after my cattle."

"Don't you mean your boss's cattle?"

"Those cattle are mine."

"*You're* a Chisholm?"

"Dawson Chisholm. And you are…?"

"Everyone calls me Jinx."

He chuckled. "I can see why."

Bronco busting, falling in love…it's all in a day's work.
Look for the rest of their story in

RUSTLED

Available July 2011 from Harlequin Intrigue
wherever books are sold.